THE
Song
OF THE
Quarkbeast

JASPER FFORDE

THE CHRONICLES OF KAZAM · BOOK TWO

THE
Song
OF THE
Quarkbeast

HARCOURT
Houghton Mifflin Harcourt
Boston   New York

Harcourt is an imprint of Houghton Mifflin
Harcourt Publishing Company.

www.hmhbooks.com

Text set in Garamond 3 Lt Std

LIBRARY OF CONGRESS CATALOGING-IN-PUBLICATION DATA
Fforde, Jasper.
The song of the Quarkbeast / Jasper Fforde.
pages cm—(The chronicles of Kazam ; book 2)
Originally published in Great Britain by Hodder & Stoughton, 2011.
Summary: In an alternate United Kingdom, King Snodd tries to control
the world by controlling magic and only sixteen-year-old Jennifer Strange,
acting manager of an employment agency for sorcerers, stands between
Snodd and his plans.
ISBN 978-0-547-73848-2
[1. Magic—Fiction. 2. Fantasy.] I. Title.
PZ7.F4443So 2013
[Fic]—dc23
2012047318

Manufactured in the United States of America
DOC 10 9 8 7 6 5 4 3 2 1
4500422568

For Maggy and Stu,
with grateful thanks for kindnesses
too numerous to mention

For every Quarkbeast

there is an equal and opposite Quarkbeast.

——Miss Boolean Smith, Sorcerer (Rtd.)

ONE

Where We Are Right Now

I work in the magic industry. I think you'll agree it's pretty glamorous: a life of spells, potions, and whispered enchantments; of levitation, vanishings, and alchemy. Of titanic fights to the death with the powers of darkness, of conjuring up blizzards and quelling storms at sea. Of casting lightning bolts from mountains, of bringing statues to life in order to vanquish troublesome foes.

If only.

No, magic these days is simply *useful,* useful in the same way that cars and dishwashers and can openers are useful. The days of wild, crowd-pleasing stuff like commanding the oceans, levitating elephants, and turning herring into taxi drivers are long gone. We had a rekindling of magic two months ago, something we called a Big Magic, but unlimited magical powers have not yet returned. After a brief surge that generated weird cloud shapes and rain that tasted of elderflower cordial, the wizidrical power had dropped to nothing before rising again almost painfully slowly. No one will be doing any ocean commanding for a while, elephants will remain unlevitated, and a herring won't lose anyone on the way to the airport. We have no foes to vanquish except the taxman, and the only time we get to fight the powers of darkness is during one of the kingdom's frequent power cuts.

So while we wait for magic to reestablish itself, it is very much business as usual: hiring out sorcerers to conduct practical magic. Things like plumbing and rewiring, wallpapering and loft conversions. We lift cars for the city's clamping unit, deliver pizza by flying carpet, and predict the weather with twenty-three percent more accuracy than SNODD-TV's favorite weather girl, Daisy Fairchild.

But I don't do any of that. I *can't* do any of that. I organize those who can. The job I do is Mystical Arts Management. Simply put, I'm an agent. The person who does the deals, takes the bookings, and then gets all the flak when things go wrong—and little of the credit when they go right. The place I do all this is a company called Kazam, the biggest House of Enchantment in the world. To be honest, that's not saying much, as there are only two: Kazam and Industrial Magic, over in Stroud. Between us we have the only eight licensed sorcerers on the planet. And if you think that's a responsible job for a sixteen-year-old, you're right—I'm really only *acting* manager until the Great Zambini gets back.

If he does.

So the day this all began, it was once again business as usual at Kazam, and this morning we were going to try to find something that was lost. Not just "Misplaced it—whoops" lost, which is easy, but never-to-be-found lost, which is a good deal harder. We didn't much like finding lost stuff, as in general lost stuff doesn't like to be found, but when work was slack, we'd do pretty much anything within the law. And that's why Perkins, Tiger, and I were sitting in my orange Volkswagen Beetle one damp autumn morning at a roadside rest area six miles from our town of Hereford, the capital city of the Kingdom of Snodd.

"Do you think a wizard even knows what a clock is *for?*" I asked, somewhat exasperated. I had promised our client that we'd start at nine thirty a.m. sharp, and it was twenty past already. I'd told the sorcerers to get here at nine o'clock for a briefing, but I might as well have been talking to the flowers.

"If you have all the time in the world," replied Tiger, referring to a sorcerer's often greatly increased life expectancy, "then I suppose a few minutes either way doesn't matter so much."

Horton "Tiger" Prawns was my assistant and had been with Kazam for two months. He was tall for his twelve years and had curly sandy-colored hair and freckles that danced around a snub nose. Like most foundlings of that age, he wore his oversized hand-me-downs with a certain pride. He was here this morning to learn the peculiar problems associated with a finding—and with good reason. If the Great Zambini took more than two years to return, Tiger would take over as acting manager. Once I turned eighteen, I'd be out.

Perkins nodded. "Some wizards do seem to live a long time," he observed. This was undoubtedly true, but they were always cagey about how they did it, and changed the subject to mice or onions or something when asked.

The Youthful Perkins was our best and only trainee wrapped up in one. He had been at Kazam just over a year and was the only person at the company close to my age. He was good-looking, too, and aside from suffering bouts of overconfidence that sometimes got him into trouble when he spelled quicker than he thought, he would be good for Kazam and good for magic in general. I liked him, but since his particular field of interest was Remote Suggestion—the skill of projecting thoughts into people's heads from a distance—I didn't know whether I actually liked him or he was *suggesting* I like him, which was both creepy and unethical. In fact, the whole Remote Suggestion or "seeding" idea had been banned once it was discovered to be the key ingredient in promoting talentless boy bands, which had until then been something of a mystery.

I looked at my watch. The sorcerers we were waiting for were the Amazing Dennis "Full" Price and Lady Mawgon. Despite their magical abilities, Mystical Arts practitioners—to give them their official title—could barely get their clothes on in the right order and often needed to be reminded to take a bath and attend meals regularly. Wizards are like that: erratic, petulant, forgetful, passionate, and *hugely* frustrating. But the one thing they aren't is boring, and after a difficult start when I first came to work here, I had come to regard them all—even the really insane ones—with a great deal of fondness.

"I should really be back at the Towers studying," said the Youthful Perkins fretfully. He had his magic license hearing that afternoon and was understandably a bit jumpy.

"You know Full Price suggested you come along to

observe," I reminded him. "Finding lost stuff is all about teamwork."

"I thought sorcerers didn't like teamwork," said Tiger, who enjoyed questions more than anything other than ice cream and waffles.

"The old days of lone wizards mixing weird potions in the top of the North Tower are over," I said. "They've got to learn to work together, and it's not just me who says it—the Great Zambini was very keen on rewriting the rule book." I looked at my watch again. "I hope they actually *do* turn up." In the Great Zambini's absence, I was the one who made the groveling apologies to any disgruntled clients—something I did more than I would have liked.

"Even so," said Perkins, "I've passed my Finding Module IV, and always found the practice hiding slipper, even when it was hidden under Mysterious X's bed."

This was true, but while finding something random like a slipper was good practice, there was more to it than that. In the Mystical Arts, there always is. The only thing you really get to figure out after a lifetime of study is that there's more stuff to figure out. Frustrating and enlightening at the same time.

"The slipper had no issues with being found," I said in an attempt to explain the unexplainable. "If something doesn't want to be found, then it's harder. The Mighty

Shandar could hide things in plain sight by simply *occluding* them from view. He demonstrated the technique most famously with an unseen elephant in the room during the 1826 World Magic Expo."

"Is that where the 'elephant in the room' expression comes from?" Tiger asked.

"Yes; his name was Daniel."

"You should be taking the magic test on my behalf," remarked Perkins gloomily. "You know a lot more than I do; there are whole tracts of the *Codex Magicalis* I haven't even read."

"I've been here three years longer than you," I pointed out, "so I'm bound to know more. But having me take your test would be like asking a person with no hands to take your piano exam."

No one knows why some people can do magic and others can't. I'm not good on the theory behind magic, other than knowing it's a fusion of science and faith, but the practical way of looking at it is this: Magic swirls about us like an invisible fog of energy that can be tapped by those gifted enough, using a variety of techniques that center on layered spelling, mumbled incantations, and a burst of concentrated thought channeled through the index fingers. The technical name for this energy is "variable electro-gravitational mutable subatomic force," which doesn't mean anything at all — confused scientists just gave it an important-sounding name so as not to lose face. The usual term is "wizidrical energy," or simply "the crackle."

"By the way," said Perkins in a breezy manner, "I've got two tickets to see Jimmy 'Daredevil' Nuttjob have himself fired from a cannon through a brick wall."

Jimmy Nuttjob was the Ununited Kingdoms' most celebrated traveling daredevil, and tickets to see his madcap stunts were much in demand. He had eaten a car tire to live orchestral accompaniment the year before; it had been a great show until he nearly choked on the valve.

"Who are you taking?" I asked, glancing at Tiger. The "Will Perkins build up the courage to ask me out?" issue had been active for a while.

Perkins cleared his throat as he built up the courage.

"You, if you want to come."

I stared at the road for a moment, then said, "Who, me?"

"Yes, of course you," said Perkins.

"You might have been talking to Tiger."

"Why would I ask Tiger to come watch a lunatic fire himself through a brick wall?"

"Why *wouldn't* you ask me?" asked Tiger. "Watching some idiot damage himself might be just my thing."

"That's entirely possible," agreed Perkins, "but as long as there's a prettier alternative, you'll always remain ninth or tenth on my list."

We all fell silent.

"Pretty?" I swiveled in the driver's seat to face him. "You want to ask me out because I'm pretty?"

"Is there a problem with asking you out because you're pretty?"

"I think you blew it," said Tiger with a grin. "You should be asking her out because she's smart, witty, mature beyond her years, and because every moment in her company makes you want to be a better person. Pretty should be at the *bottom* of the list."

"Oh, blast," said Perkins despondently. "It should, shouldn't it?"

"At last!" I muttered, hearing the distinctive *dugadugadugaduga* of Lady Mawgon's motorcycle, and we climbed out of the car as she came to a stop. She was wearing her "I'm about to harangue Jennifer" sort of look. Of course, being harangued by Lady Mawgon was nothing new; I was often harangued by her at lunch, dinner, and random times in between. She was our most powerful sorcerer, and also the crabbiest. She was so crabby, in fact, that even really crabby people put their crabbiness aside to write her gushing yet mildly sarcastic fan letters.

"Lady Mawgon," I said in a bright voice, bowing low, as protocol dictated. "I trust the day finds you well?"

"An idiotic expression made acceptable only because it is adrift in a sea of equally idiotic expressions," she muttered grumpily, stepping from the motorcycle that she rode sidesaddle. "Is that little twerp attempting to hide behind what you jokingly refer to as a car?"

"Good morning," said Tiger in his best *Gosh, didn't see you there, I wasn't really hiding* voice. "You are looking *most* well this morning."

Tiger was lying. Lady Mawgon looked terrible, with lank hair and a sour, pinched face. Her lips had never seen a smile and rarely passed an intentional friendly word. She was dressed in a long black bell-shaped crinoline dress that buttoned up to her throat in one direction and swept the floor in the other. She didn't so much walk as *glide* across the ground in a very disturbing manner. Tiger had once bet me half a moolah that she wore roller skates; trouble was, neither of us could think of a good, safe, or respectful way to find out.

She greeted Perkins more politely, as he was of the wizidrical calling. She didn't waste a salutation on Tiger or me. Yet despite our low status as foundlings, Tiger and I were crucial to the smooth running of Kazam. It was how the Great Zambini liked it. He always felt that foundlings were better equipped to deal with the somewhat bizarre world of Mystical Arts Management. "Pampered civilians," as he put it, "would panic at the weirdness, or think they know better, or try to improve things, or get greedy and try to cash in." He was probably right.

"While you're here," announced Lady Mawgon, "I need to run a test spell later this morning."

"How many shandars, ma'am?"

"About ten megashandars," said Lady Mawgon sullenly, annoyed at the ignominy of having to run her test spells past me first.

"That's a considerable amount of crackle." I wondered what she was up to and hoped she wouldn't attempt to bring her cat, Mr. Pusskins, back to some sort of semi-life, an act not only *seriously* creepy but highly frowned upon. "May I inquire as to what you are planning to do?"

"I'm going to try and hack into the Dibble Storage Coils. It may help us with the bridge job."

I breathed a sigh of relief. This changed matters considerably, and she was right. We had agreed to rebuild Hereford's medieval bridge on Friday, and we needed all the help we could get. That was why Perkins was taking his magic test today rather than next week. He'd still be a novice, but six licensed sorcerers would be better than five—magic always worked better with the wizards in use divisible by three.

"Let me see," I said, consulting my schedule. Two sorcerers spelling at the same time could deplete the crackle, and there is nothing worse than running out of steam two-thirds of the way through a spell. A bit like running out of gas within sight of a filling station.

"At eleven o'clock the Price brothers are moving the zoo's prize walrus, so anytime after eleven fifteen would be good — but I'll double-check with Industrial Magic just in case."

"Eleven fifteen it is," replied Lady Mawgon stonily. "You may observe, if you so choose."

"I'll be there," I replied, then added cautiously, "Lady Mawgon, please don't think me insensitive, but any attempt to reanimate Mr. Pusskins on the back of the Dibble Storage Coil hacking enchantment might be looked on unfavorably by the other wizards."

Her eyes narrowed and she gave me one of those stares that seem to hit the back of my skull like a dozen hot needles.

"None of you have any idea what Mr. Pusskins meant to me. Now, what are we doing here?"

"Waiting for the Amazing Dennis Price."

"How I deplore poor timekeeping," she said, despite being almost half an hour late herself. "Got any money? I'm starving."

Perkins gave her a one-moolah coin.

"Most kind. Walk with me, Perkins." And she glided silently off toward a roadside snack bar at the other end of the rest area.

"Do you want anything?" asked Perkins.

"Eating out gives foundlings ideas above their station," came Lady Mawgon's decisive voice, quickly followed by an admonishment to the owner of the snack bar: "*That* much for a bacon roll? Scandalous!"

"Since when is a roadside snack bar eating out?" said Tiger, leaning against the car. "That's like saying listening to the radio outdoors is like going to a live show."

"She is an astonishing sorceress of considerable power and commitment, so don't be impertinent. Or at least," I added, "not within earshot."

"Speaking of live shows," said Tiger, lowering his voice, "will you go to Jimmy 'Daredevil' Nuttjob's stunt show with Perkins?"

"Probably not," I said with a sigh. "It's not a good idea to date someone you work with."

"Good," said Tiger.

"Why is that good?"

"Because he might give away your ticket, and I'd like to watch someone with more bravery than sense being fired from a cannon into a brick wall."

"Is there a warm-up act?"

"A brass band, cheerleaders, and someone who can juggle bobcats."

We turned to see a taxi approaching. It was the Amazing Dennis "Full" Price, another one of our licensed operatives. He and his brother, David, known as Half Price, were famous as the most unidentical twins on record. David was tall and thin and would sway in a high wind, while Dennis was short and squat like a giant pink pumpkin. After I paid for the taxi, he climbed out and looked around.

"Sorry I'm late," Full Price said, demonstrating the difference between him and Lady Mawgon. "I got delayed talking to Wizard Moobin. He wants you to witness an experiment he's got cooking."

"A dangerous one?" I asked with some concern. Wizard Moobin had destroyed more laboratories than I'd had cold and inedible dinners.

"Does he know any other?" Price replied. "Where's Mawgon?"

I nodded in the direction of the snack bar.

"Not with her own money, I'll bet," he said, and after giving us a wink, he strode off to talk to her.

As Tiger and I stood there smelling the faint aroma of frying bacon on the breeze, a Rolls-Royce whispered to a halt next to us.

In Pursuit of Lost Stuff

The Rolls-Royce was a top-of-the-line six-wheeled Phantom Twelve. It was as big as a yacht and twice as luxurious, and had paint work so perfect, the vehicle looked like a pool of black paint sitting in the air. The chauffeur opened the rear passenger door, and a well-dressed girl climbed out. She was not much older than I was, but she came from a world of privilege, cash, and entitlement. I should have hated her, but I didn't.

I envied her.

"Miss Strange?" she said, striding confidently forward, hand outstretched. "Miss Shard is glad to make your acquaintance."

"Who's she talking about?" asked Tiger under his breath, looking around.

"Herself, I think." I smiled broadly to welcome her. "Good morning, Miss Shard. Thank you for coming. I'm Jennifer Strange."

This was our client. She didn't look old enough to have lost something important enough to call us, but you never knew.

"One must call me Ann," she said kindly. "Your recent exploits of a magical variety filled one with a sense of thrilling trepidation."

She was talking in Longspeak, the formal language of the upper classes, and it seemed that she was not fluent in Shortspeak, the everyday language of the Ununited Kingdoms.

"I'm sorry?"

"It was a singular display of inspired audaciousness," she replied.

"Is that good?" I asked, still unsure of her meaning.

"Most certainly," she replied. "We followed your adventures with great interest."

"We?"

"Myself and my client. A gentleman of some consequence, sagacity, and countenance."

She was undoubtedly referring to someone of nobility. Royals in the Ununited Kingdoms employed others to do almost everything for them; only the very poorest nobles did anything for themselves. It was said that when King Wozzle of Snowdonia tired of eating, he employed someone to do it for him. After the inevitable weight loss and death, he was succeeded by his brother.

"I can't understand a word she's saying," whispered Tiger.

"Tiger," I said, keen to get rid of him before she took offense, "why not fetch Full Price and Lady Mawgon, hmm?"

"Were they of a disingenuous countenance?" Miss Shard asked, smiling politely.

"Were who of what?"

"The dragons," she said. "Were they . . . unpleasant?"

"Not really," I replied, guarded. I had some history with dragons, and almost everyone wanted to know about them. I revealed little; dragons value discretion more than anything. I said nothing more, and she got the message.

"I defer to your circumspection on this issue," she replied with a slight bow.

"O . . . kay," I said, not really getting that, either. "This is the team."

Tiger had returned with Full Price and Lady Mawgon, followed by Perkins in his observing capacity. I introduced them all, and Miss Shard said something about how it was "entirely convivial" and "felicitous" to meet them on "this auspicious occasion," and in return they shook hands but remained wary. It pays to distance oneself from clients, especially ones who use too many long words.

"What do you want us to find?" asked Lady Mawgon, who always got straight to the point.

"It's a ring that belonged to the mother of my client," the girl said. "He would be here personally to present his request but finds himself unavailable due to a prolonged sabbatical."

"Has he seen a doctor about it?" asked Tiger.

"About what?"

"His prolonged sabbatical. It sounds very painful."

She stared at him for a moment. "It means he's on vacation."

"Oh."

"I apologize for the ignorance of the staff," said Lady Mawgon, glaring at Tiger, "but Kazam sadly requires foundling labor to function. Staff can be so difficult these days, wanting frivolous little luxuries like food, shoes, wages . . . and human dignity."

"Please don't worry," said Miss Shard politely. "Foundlings can be refreshingly direct sometimes."

"About the ring?" I asked, uncomfortable with all this talk of foundlings.

"Nothing remarkable," replied Miss Shard. "Gold, plain, large like a thumb ring. My client is eager to present it to his mother as a seventieth birthday gift."

"Not a problem," remarked Full Price. "Do you have anything that might have been in contact with this ring?"

"Such as your client's mother?" said Tiger in an impish manner.

"There's this," replied Miss Shard, producing a ring from her pocket. "This was on her middle finger, and rubbed against the lost ring. You can observe the marks. Look."

Lady Mawgon took the ring and stared at it intently for a moment before she clenched it in her fist, murmured something, and then opened her hand. The ring hovered an inch above her open palm, revolving slowly. She passed it to Full Price, who held it up to the light and then popped it into his mouth, clicked it against his fillings for a moment, and then swallowed it.

"Meant to do that," he said in the tone of someone who didn't.

"Really?" asked Miss Shard dubiously, surely wondering how she was going to get it back and in what condition.

"Don't worry," said Price cheerfully. "Amazing how powerful cleaning agents are these days."

"Why did you ask us to meet you here?" asked Lady Mawgon.

It was a good question. We were at an unremarkable rest area on the Ross-Hereford Road near a village called Harewood End.

"This is where she lost it," replied Miss Shard. "It was in her possession when she egressed from her vehicle, and when she departed she didn't have it anymore."

Lady Mawgon looked at me, then at our client, then at Full Price. She smelled the air, mumbled something, and looked thoughtful for a moment.

"This ring is still around here somewhere," she said, "and it's been lost for thirty-two years, ten months, and nine days. Am I correct?"

Miss Shard stared at her. It appeared this was indeed true, and it was impressive. Mawgon had picked up the lingering memory that human emotion can instill on even the most inert of objects.

"Something that stays lost that long is lost for a good reason," added Full Price. "Why doesn't your client give his mother some chocolates instead?"

"Or flowers," said Lady Mawgon. "We can't help you. Good day." She turned to move away.

"We'll pay you a thousand moolah."

Lady Mawgon stopped. A thousand moolah was serious cash.

"A thousand?"

"My client is inclined toward generosity regarding his mother."

Lady Mawgon looked at Full Price, then at me.

"Five thousand," she said.

"Five thousand?" echoed Ann Shard. "To find a ring?"

"This ring *shouldn't* be found," replied Lady Mawgon. "The price reflects the risks."

Miss Shard looked at us all in turn.

"I accept," she said at last, "and I will wait here for results. But no find, no fee. Not even a call-out charge."

"We usually charge for an attempt—" I began, but Mawgon cut me short.

"We're agreed," she said, and made a grimace that might have been her version of a smile.

Miss Shard shook hands with each of us again and climbed back into her Rolls-Royce, and a few seconds later the limousine moved off to park opposite the snack bar. The allure of a bacon sandwich observed no class barriers.

"With the greatest respect," I said, turning to Lady Mawgon, "if it gets around that we've been fleecing clients, Kazam's reputation will plummet. And what's more, I think it's unprofessional."

"How can civilians hate us any more than they already do?" she asked disdainfully. She had a point. Despite our best efforts, the general public still regarded the magic trade with grave suspicion. "More important," added Lady Mawgon, "I've seen the accounts. How long do you think we can give our skills away for free? Besides, she's in a Phantom Eight. Loaded with moolah."

"It's a Phantom Twelve," murmured Tiger.

"Shall we get a move on?" said Full Price. "I've got to move a walrus in an hour, and if I'm late, David will start without me."

"The sooner the better," said Lady Mawgon, dismissing Tiger and me with a sweep of her hand. We leaned against the car and watched as Perkins circled Mawgon and Price in an attempt to hear what was going on.

"Is Perkins going to get his license, do you think?" Tiger asked.

"He'd better. We need him for the bridge job. Fumble that and we'll all look a bit stupid."

"And on live TV, too."

"Don't remind me."

Our concerns about Perkins were valid when you consider that the license was granted by the one person more boneheaded and corrupt than our glorious ruler, King Snodd: his Useless Brother, the Minister for Infernal Affairs, the less-than-polite term used to describe the office that dealt with all things magical.

"You swallowed it!" we heard Lady Mawgon demand angrily. "Why in Snorff's name would you do something like that?" She must have meant the ring, and since there wasn't any real answer to this, Full Price just shrugged. I walked up, ready to mediate if required. Mawgon put out her hand.

"Hand it over, Dennis."

Full Price looked annoyed but knew better than to argue. He closed his eyes and took a deep breath, then made a series of odd facial expressions and huffy exertion noises before rolling up his sleeve. The shape of the ring *beneath* the skin moved down his forearm, and he sweated and grunted with the effort. I had seen this done several times before, the most recent to expel a bullet lodged perilously close to a patient's spine, the result of a shooting accident.

"Ah!" said Full Price, as the ring-shaped lump moved across the top of his hand. "Ow, ow, *ow!*"

The ring traveled down the tighter skin of his finger and rotated around his fingertip. After a lot of swearing, Price succeeded in expelling it from under his nail bed.

"That is so gross," said Tiger.

"I agree," replied Perkins, "but it's sort of impossible not to look, don't you think?"

"There," said Full Price, wiping off the ring and handing it to Mawgon. "Happy now?"

But Lady Mawgon was already thinking of other things. She took the ring, murmured something around it, and handed it back to Price, who held it tightly in his fist.

"I don't like the feel of this," he said. "Something bad happened."

"I agree," replied Mawgon, taking out a small crystal bottle with a silver stopper. Tiger and I had stepped back to allow them to work, and Perkins, now fully mystified by what was going on, had joined us.

"They'll try to animate the memory," I said.

"Gold has a memory?"

"Everything has a memory. Gold's memory is quite tedious—got mined, got crushed, went to the smelters, got banged with a hammer—big yawn. No, we're looking for a stronger memory that has been induced onto the gold. The recollections of the person wearing the ring."

"You can transfer your memories to inanimate objects?"

"Certainly. And the stronger you feel about something, the longer the memory will stick around. The more something is loved, enjoyed, and valued, the stronger the memory and the more we can read into it."

"And the crystal bottle?"

"Watch and learn."

Lady Mawgon placed a single drop on the ring that Full Price was holding, and in an instant the ring morphed into a small dog. It ran around for a bit, wagging its tail and barking. It sparkled slightly and seemed to be made of solid gold.

"Good boy," said Lady Mawgon. "Find it."

The small memory-dog gave a low bark and scuttled off, sniffing the ground this way and that as it tried to remember where the ring might have gone. Lady Mawgon and Full Price followed the dog away from the road, opened a gate, and then chased it across a field, much to the amusement of several cows. We all followed, stopping occasionally as the memory-dog paused to think for a while or scratch its ear with a hind leg, then chased off in another direction. It would often double back on itself as it tried to catch the memory-scent, all the while with Lady Mawgon's index finger steadily pointed at it. Once, it thought its tail was the quarry and snapped at it, then realized its mistake and moved on.

"Speaking of lost, I wonder what happened to my luggage," said Tiger as we followed the sorcerers and the dog across the field, over a stile and a smaller road, then into a small wood.

"What luggage?"

"My red suitcase with wheels and a separate internal pocket for toiletries," replied Tiger. "I lost it on an orphanage trip. Luckily, it didn't have anything in it. The luggage was my only possession. It was what I was found in."

Owning very little — or even being found in a red suitcase with wheels and a separate internal pocket for toiletries — was not unusual when you considered Tiger's foundling heritage. He had been abandoned on the steps of the Sisterhood of the Blessed Ladies of the Lobster the same as I had, then sold into servitude with Kazam Mystical Arts Management until he turned eighteen. I still had two years to go before I could apply for citizenship; Tiger had six.

We didn't complain, because this was how things were. There were a lot of orphans due to the hideously wasteful and annoyingly frequent Troll Wars, and hotels, fast food joints, and laundries needed the cheap labor that foundlings could provide. Of the twenty-three kingdoms, duchies, socialist collectives, public limited companies, and ramshackle potentates that made up the Ununited Kingdoms, only three had outlawed the trade in foundlings. Unluckily for us, the Kingdom of Snodd was not one of them.

"When we have some surplus crackle, we'll retrieve your luggage," I said, knowing how valuable any connection to parents was to a foundling. I had been left on the front seat of the Volkswagen Beetle that I still own, and little would part me from my car.

"It's okay," Tiger said with the selflessness and humility of most foundlings. "It can wait."

We followed Mawgon, Full Price, and the memory-dog out of the small wood and through a gate into an abandoned farm. Brambles, creepers, and hazel saplings had grown over many of the red-brick buildings, and rusty machinery stood in sagging barns with dilapidated roofs. The memory-dog ran across the yard and stopped at an old well, where it wagged its tail excitedly. As soon as Lady Mawgon caught up, she made a flourish; the dog chased its tail until it was nothing more than a golden blur, then turned back into the ring, which continued spinning on a flagstone with a curious humming noise.

Lady Mawgon picked up the ring and gave it back to me. It was still warm and smelled of puppies. Full Price pulled a weathered door off the wellhead, and we all gazed down the brick-lined walls. Far below in the inky blackness I could see a small circle of sky and the silhouettes of our heads as our reflections stared back up at us.

"It's in there," Mawgon said.

"And there it should stay," replied Full Price, who still wasn't happy. "I can feel something wrong."

"How wrong?" I asked.

"Seventh circle of wrong. I can sense the lingering aftertaste of an old spell, too."

There was silence for a moment as everyone took this in, and a coldness seemed to emanate up from the well.

"I can sense something, too," said Perkins, "like that feeling you get when someone you don't like is looking over your shoulder."

"The ring doesn't want to be found," said Full Price.

"No," said Perkins, "*someone* doesn't want it to be found."

Missing objects are one thing, but hidden objects are quite another.

"I can think of five thousand good reasons to find it," said Lady Mawgon, "so find it we shall."

THREE

Magnaflux Reversal

Lady Mawgon put her hand above the well in order to draw the ring from the mud below, but instead of the ring rising, her hand was tugged sharply downward.

"It's been anchored and resists my command," she said, her voice tinged with intrigue. "Mr. Price?"

They both attempted to lift the ring from the well. But no sooner had they started the lift than a low rumble seemed to come from the earth beneath our feet and the bricks that made up the low wall started to shift. Tiger and I took a step back, but the others simply watched as an old and long-forgotten enchantment moved the bricks into a new configuration, sealing the wellhead tight. Within a few seconds there was only a solid brick cap.

"Fascinating," said Lady Mawgon, for this was in effect a battle of wits between sorcerers, separated by thirty years. Whatever enchantment had been left to keep the ring hidden, it was still powerful.

"I vote we walk away now," said Full Price.

"It's a challenge," replied Lady Mawgon excitedly, "and I like a challenge."

She was more animated than I had seen her for a while, and within a few minutes she had formulated a plan.

"Right, then," she said. "Listen closely. Mr. Price is going to pry open the wellhead using a standard Magnaflux Reversal. How long can you keep it open, Dennis?"

Full Price sucked air in through his teeth thoughtfully. "About thirty seconds—maximum forty."

"Should be enough. But since the ring is *resisting* a lift, we will have to send someone down to get it. I will levitate them head downward to the bottom of the well, where they will retrieve the ring. You, Mr. Perkins, will channel crackle to Mr. Price and myself. Can you do that?"

"To the best of my ability, ma'am," replied Perkins happily. Lady Mawgon had never asked him to assist her before.

"He doesn't have a license," I said. "You know what the penalty could be."

"Who's going to snitch on him?" she retorted. "You?"

"I can't allow it," I said.

"It's Perkins's call," said Mawgon, looking at me angrily. "Mr. Perkins?"

Perkins looked at me and then at Lady Mawgon. "I'll do it."

I didn't say anything more, but we all knew the consequences of operating without a license were extremely unpleasant. The relationship between the populace and Mystical Arts practitioners had always been one of suspicion, not helped by a regrettable episode in the nineteenth century when a wayward sorcerer who called himself Blix the Thoroughly Barbarous thought he could use his powers to achieve world domination. He was eventually defeated, but the damage to magic's reputation had been deep and far-reaching. Bureaucracy now dominated the industry with a sea of paperwork and licensing requirements. Reinventing sorcery as a useful and safe commodity akin to electricity had taken two centuries and wasn't finished yet. Once lost, trust is a difficult thing to regain. But I said nothing more. I was there to remind them of the rules, not to police them.

"Good," said Lady Mawgon. "Then let's begin."

"Wait a minute," said Tiger, who had just figured

out that the going-down-a-well-headfirst plan included him. He was the smallest. "It's going to be as dark as the belly of a whale down there."

I took a glass globe from my bag, just one of the many useful objects that I liked to have with me on assignment.

"It runs off sarcasm," I said, handing it to him.

"Great," Tiger replied, and the globe lit up brightly.

"You'll also need this," I told him as I positioned a baby shoe against his ear and tied its laces around his neck. I spoke into the matching shoe in my hand. "Can you hear me?"

"Yes," he replied, "I can hear you. Do I *have* to go down a well upside down while being sarcastic with a shoe tied around my neck?"

"You could use a conch to talk," said Perkins helpfully, then added less than helpfully, "only we haven't got any."

"And you'd look pretty silly with a conch tied to your head," added Full Price.

"Like I am so not worried about looking like a twit," said Tiger, and the globe went to full brightness again.

"You're going to have to find the ring within thirty seconds," announced Lady Mawgon, "and since it might be tricky to find in the rank, fetid, disease-ridden muddy water, you'll need my help."

"You're coming down, too?"

"Good Lord, no. What do you think I am? An idiot?"

"I'm not sure it would be healthy for me to answer that question," replied Tiger carefully.

"Answer it how you want — I'd ignore you anyway. Here."

She handed him a neat leather glove and told him to put it on while she placed its mate on herself. Like baby shoes and conches, gloves have left-and-right symmetry and can thus work together while separated by physical distance. Lady Mawgon clenched and unclenched her fist as Tiger's hand did the same. She revolved her arm in the air, and the other glove copied her actions perfectly while Tiger stared at his arm and hand. He was, for all intents and purposes, now partly Lady Mawgon. Better still, the gloves were feedback-enabled. Lady Mawgon's hand would feel what Tiger was feeling.

"How's that?" asked Lady Mawgon.

"Peculiar," he replied. "What if I can't find the blasted ring in thirty seconds?"

"Then the bricks will close and it's entirely possible you'll spend the rest of your life at the bottom of a deep well with only bacteria and leeches for company, then utter darkness when your sarcasm runs out."

"I'm not so sure I want to do this anymore."

"Don't be such a crybaby," chided Lady Mawgon. "If

our roles were reversed and you were the skilled practitioner and I was the worthless foundling with the silly name, I'd be down that hole like an actor after a free lunch."

Tiger looked across at me and raised an eyebrow.

"You don't have to do this if you don't want to," I told him.

"Lady Mawgon is relating a worst-case scenario," said Full Price in a soothing voice. "We'll call the fire brigade if we can't reopen the well. The longest you'll be trapped is an hour."

"Then how could I possibly refuse?" replied Tiger grumpily. "Let's get on with it."

Lady Mawgon and Full Price took up their stances, index fingers at the ready. At the count of three, Full Price pointed at the wellhead and the bricks opened again, revealing the deep hole. At the same time, Lady Mawgon pointed at Tiger and my young assistant was lifted from the ground, turned upside down, and plunged headfirst down the well.

We peered over to look in. It was all dark until Tiger said, "Gosh, what super fun this is," and the globe lit up to reveal the brick-lined well all the way down. After a few moments Tiger's voice came through the shoe, telling me that he was at the bottom and that it was wet and muddy and very smelly and all he could see was an old bicycle and a shopping cart.

"They get everywhere," I said. "Let Lady Mawgon have a feel around."

Mawgon already was. While one hand kept Tiger floating a few inches above the water level, the other was grasping, feeling, and churning above her head; the glove on Tiger's hand sixty feet below did the same thing. Tiger kept us informed of what was going on, interspersing his speech with some top-quality sarcasm.

"Fifteen seconds gone," I said, staring at my watch.

"I can feel something odd," said Perkins, who was standing to one side, doing little except directing the ambient crackle more efficiently into Mawgon and Price, the same way a gutter directs rain into a storm drain.

"Me, too," said Full Price, eyes fixed intently on the wellhead as his index fingers began to vibrate with the effort. "Look at that."

I looked down the well. Before, only the top layer of bricks had closed over, but now other bricks were popping out from the sides of the well all the way down. The well was starting to constrict.

"We need Tiger out!" I said to Lady Mawgon, who was still feeling above her head as she searched the muddy bottom of the well.

"Nearly," she muttered, eyes closed.

"Twenty-five seconds! Five seconds left!"

"What's going on?" came Tiger's voice over the baby shoe.

"You'll be out soon, Tiger, I promise."

The bricks were moving in with increased speed, and brick dust, soil, and earwigs were tumbling down the well. Full Price was sweating with effort and shaking badly.

"*I . . . can't . . . hold . . . it!*" he managed to mutter between clenched teeth.

"The walls," came Tiger's tremulous voice. "They're moving in!"

"Lady Mawgon," I said as calmly as I could. "It's only a ring. We can leave it be."

"Almost there," she said, feeling around with her gloved hand in increased desperation.

"Thirty seconds," I said. "That's it. Abort."

Lady Mawgon continued on, undeterred.

"Mawgon!" yelled Full Price, who was now shaking so hard his index fingers were a blur. "Get the lad out *now!*"

But she was unmoved, so intent on finding her quarry that nothing mattered—least of all a foundling being crushed to death by an ancient spell sixty feet underground. The well had shrunk to half its width by now, and Full Price was crying out in pain as he tried to keep the spell at bay. Perkins was shaking with the effort, too, and Lady Mawgon was still wildly feeling around when several things happened at once. She cried out, Perkins fell over, and the well shut with a teeth-jarring *thump* that we felt through the ground.

I looked at my watch. Price had kept the well open for exactly forty-three seconds. It was now a solid plug of brick, and down below, somewhere, Tiger was part of it.

Negative Energy

No one spoke. Full Price and Perkins were both on their hands and knees in the dirt coughing after their exertions, but Lady Mawgon was just standing there, her gloved hand half open as if clasped around something. She might have found something, but it didn't matter. The price had been too great.

My head grew hot as anger welled up inside of me. I might have boiled over, even though I work very hard to control my temper. But a small voice brought me back from the edge.

"Hey, Jenny," it said from the baby shoe. "I can see Zambini Towers from here."

It was Tiger. I frowned and then looked up. High

above us was a small figure no bigger than a dot, free-falling back toward earth. Lady Mawgon had brought Tiger out of the closing well so rapidly that we hadn't seen him pass; he had continued on up and was now on his way back down. I looked across at Lady Mawgon, who winked at me. She swiftly moved a hay cart twenty feet to the right, where Tiger landed with a thump a few seconds later, and at the same time she caught a muddy object in her gloved hand.

"There," she said with a triumphant grin as she passed the object to me. "Mawgon delivers."

"That was fun in a panicky, exciting, soil-your-underwear kind of way," said Tiger as he walked up to us covered in a mixture of mud and straw. "I *didn't,* in case you're interested. The smell is the mud from the bottom of the well."

Full Price was the first to voice what we all felt.

"Cutting it a bit close, Daphne?"

"I knew *precisely* how long he had," Lady Mawgon said. "Master Prawns was never in danger."

"I don't agree," I replied, pointing to where a lock of Tiger's hair must have been torn out as the bricks closed upon him. "I'll ask you not to place the staff in danger, Lady Mawgon."

She stared at me and took a step closer.

"You *admonish* me?" she said with great deliberation. "You, who are not worthy to even carry my bag? We'll see where the land lies when the Great Zambini returns, my girl. Prawns was in slight jeopardy, yes, but as an employee at Kazam he must assume the risks as well as the advantages."

"And what would those advantages be?" asked Tiger, who clearly thought he could be impertinent, given his recent close shave. "I'd be very interested in knowing."

"Isn't it obvious?" she replied. "Working with the greatest practitioners of the Mystical Arts currently on the earth."

"*Aside* from that," replied Tiger, as that was something we could all agree upon.

"What else does there need to be? Clean my glove before you return it to me. I just earned the company five thousand moolah. You should all be mind-numbingly grateful."

"Why would anyone leave such a strong spell just to keep a ring hidden?" asked Perkins, artfully moving the conversation to where it should have been.

No one had any good answer. I looked at the small mud-covered terra cotta pot Lady Mawgon had handed me. It was about the size of a pear, the sort of thing you might use to hold mixed spices. I put my finger in the neck and felt around in the muddy gloop until I pulled out the gold ring, still shiny and perfect after thirty years down the well. It was a large ring for a large finger but was otherwise unremarkable. No inscription or anything, just a simple band of gold.

Full Price put his hand out, then hurriedly withdrew it. "It's suffused with negative wizidrical energy — a jumble of hateful and hurtful emotions. It remembers violence and betrayal. It's cursed."

"That would explain all those creepy feelings," said Perkins with a grimace.

Everyone took a cautious step back. Curses were the viruses of the magical world — mischievous strands of negative emotional energy wrapped up in nastiness, waiting to pounce and ensnare the unwary. They'd attach to anything and anybody and were the devil's own job to remove. It was Lady Mawgon who broke the uneasy silence.

"What are we worrying about?" she said. "Five thousand moolah is five thousand moolah. Besides, it's none of our business. And what's new about a curse? The country is littered with redundant strands of curse spells left over from past suffering."

This was all too true. The sometimes violent history of the Ununited Kingdoms had seeded the ground with spells cast when something terrible had happened. They could pop back to life with something as simple as digging in the garden. One moment you're planting spuds and thinking of dinner, and the next you're taking cover from a shower of pitchforks.

"The public can take their chances like the rest of us," added Lady Mawgon. "Are you suggesting that all we've been through this morning should be ignored in case we inadvertently pass on the *possibility* of a curse?"

"Odd as it may seem," said Tiger, feeling where the hair was missing from the top of his head, "I am in agreement with Lady Mawgon on that count."

"A rare moment of clarity from someone usually confined only to stupidities," remarked Lady Mawgon. "Our work here is done."

She was right. We returned to the rest area in silence, and Lady Mawgon departed on her motorcycle without another word. I sighed. Earning one's keep by magic was rarely smooth sailing. For every simple job there were others like this. If the ring had a potential curse, then its return would definitely cause unpleasantness for Miss Shard or anyone associated with it. Then again, five grand would support Kazam's key function: the dignity and majesty of the Mystical Arts. But then again, where was the dignity in just finding lost stuff and doing loft conversions? And as Lady Mawgon had said, it was none of our business.

I walked up to where the Rolls-Royce was still parked, the gold ring in the palm of my hand. I tapped on the tinted window, which lowered with a hum.

"Did the finding exercise meet with a modicum of positive fortitude?" asked Miss Shard.

"Pardon?"

"Did you find it?"

I paused for a moment and held the ring tightly in my fist.

"I'm afraid not," I said, returning the other ring, the one she had loaned us. "Please offer our apologies to your client. We did all we could."

"No hints at all as to where it might be?" she asked, mildly surprised.

"None at all," I replied. "It's been more than thirty years, after all."

"Well," said Miss Shard, "I'm grateful to you nonetheless. Perhaps my client will look for it personally when he returns."

And after Miss Shard bade me good day, the Rolls-Royce purred out of the rest area, joined the morning traffic, and headed off. I watched the car go with an odd feeling of foreboding. About what, I wasn't sure. I popped the ring back into the pot and wedged my handkerchief in as a stopper.

As we drove back into town without the five grand, I considered my decision. I had done the right thing. The power Kazam had was power abused if we didn't accept responsibility for any adverse outcomes, and spell curses would damage our already poor standing. I smiled to myself. I think it's what the Great Zambini would have done.

All in all, it had been quite a morning.

FIVE

Zambini Towers

I parked the car in the yard behind Zambini Towers. After telling Tiger to go take a shower to remove the stinking mud, I made my way through the building. In more glory-scented days Zambini Towers had been the Majestic Hotel, one of only four hotels to ever host the coveted Despot of the Decade award ceremony. It had been featured in *What Hotel?* magazine as the most luxurious hotel to be found in the lesser kingdoms, where, it noted, "food poisoning was likely but by no means a certainty."

That was then. Today the Majestic was both Kazam's headquarters and a shabby relic far removed from its former glory. The ballroom, where once B-list princes wooed their consorts to the dulcet tones of string quartets, was now a dining room that smelled strongly of burned toast and damp. The presidential suite, long ago the playground for an exotic array of noblemen, was these days the dwelling place of the Mysterious X, who was less of a who and more of a what—with peculiar and borderline-disgusting personal habits.

I passed through the lobby, where the gnarled boughs of a mature oak tree wrapped tightly around the furniture and ornate cast-iron railings of what had once been the lobby café. Half Price had grown the oak as a first-year student project twenty years earlier but had never gotten around to ungrowing it.

I walked into the Kazam offices, flicked on the light, dumped my bag onto a chair, and put the small terra cotta pot in my desk drawer. This office was the nerve center of the company, and a half century ago, during the days of full-power magic, it had hummed with action as thirty or so managers fielded calls and scheduled enchantments. The desks were all empty these days, but we kept the furniture and telephones just to remind ourselves how good it had once been and, if we had our way, would be again.

I sat down at my desk, thought for a moment about the morning's adventure, made a few notes on my pad, then picked up the phone and dialed a number from memory.

"iMagic," came a snotty voice on the other end, "better, faster, and cheaper than Kazam and home to the All Powerful Blix. Can I help you?"

"That's not helpful, Gladys," I said. Competition had become fiercer between the two companies since the Big Magic, but at least we at Kazam never stooped to badmouthing the opposition.

"Only speaking the truth, Jennifer," she sneered. "I'll get the All Power—I mean, the Amazing Blix for you."

Conrad Blix was not only the chief wizard over at Industrial Magic but also general manager, doing what I did here at Kazam. The Great Zambini had disliked Blix intensely, and not just because he was the grandson of the infamous Blix the Hideously Barbarous but also because they had never seen eye to eye about the direction of the Mystical Arts. Zambini saw magic as a tool for social justice and good in general, but Blix saw it more as a way to make cash, and lots of it.

"Strange by name, Strange by nature," came a supercilious voice. "I'm busy, dear girl, so better make it quick."

Despite the animosity between the two companies, we were compelled to agree on a number of matters to be able to function at all. We all drew our power from the same wizidrical energy source, and any usage above five thousand shandars was worth a phone call.

"What's with the iMagic name change?" I said.

"Industrial Magic was a bit of a mouthful," Blix explained. "Besides, putting *i* in front of anything makes it more hip and current. Is that why you called?"

"No. We've got a ten-megashandar spell cooking at eleven fifteen this morning, and I wanted to make sure we wouldn't clash."

"We've got nothing big on until half past four this afternoon," replied Blix suspiciously. "What are you up to? Ten meg is a serious chunk of crackle to be using on short notice."

"You weren't jamming us yesterday, were you?" I asked, ignoring his question and referring to some interference we'd had at a routine scaffold build the previous afternoon.

"Jennifer, when you say things like that, you really hurt me," retorted Blix insincerely. "We are a professional outfit, and accusations of jamming insult our integrity."

"If a shred of integrity fell into your soul, it would die a very lonely death."

"One day I will make you eat your impertinence, Jennifer—and you won't enjoy it. Anything else?"

"Actually, there is. Since when did your accolade jump from 'the Amazing' to 'the All Powerful'?"

Accolades were self-conferring, and making yourself seem more astounding than you were was not against any written rules, but it was bad manners. Sorcerers were big on dignity and honor—or were meant to be, anyway.

"I can't think how that happened," he replied innocently. "I'll speak to Gladys about it."

"I'm most grateful. And don't forget that we want a clear hour at two o'clock for Perkins's license application."

"Already in the schedule, dear girl. In fact, I might even see you there."

"That would be joyous."

"You're very disrespectful, Jennifer."

"Mr. Zambini made me promise. *Sandop kale n'baaa,* Amazing Blix."

"*Sandop kale n'baaa,* Miss Strange."

And having exchanged the ancient salutation required of us, we both hung up. I thought for a moment. If Blix was attempting to accolade himself All Powerful, there might be trouble brewing. Wizards on a self-aggrandizing kick usually set the alarm bells ringing.

"Do you think Blix will try to sabotage Perkins's application?" asked Tiger, rubbing his damp hair with a towel as he walked in.

"I wouldn't put it past him. Samantha 'Pretty-but-Dim' Flynt has failed to get her license for three years running, and Perkins's success would really piss them off."

"Cadet Flynt couldn't find her foot without tattooed arrows running down her leg," said Tiger, "and she failed her basic practical-skills test. I don't know why they bother."

"Hopeless she might be," I said, "but she's dazzlingly pretty, and Blix thinks that a physically attractive sorcerer would be good for his business."

"She'd certainly be unique," remarked Tiger. Sorcerers are not known for their good looks.

"In any event, we should be on our guard with Blix. I wouldn't trust him farther than Patrick of Ludlow could throw him."

Patrick was our heavy lifter. His specialty was moving objects, now mostly illegally parked cars for the city. He had a heart of gold and was as gentle as a lamb, despite his power and odd appearance.

"I'd like to see Patrick try, though."

"Me, too. Hello, Hector."

The Transient Moose had suddenly materialized over by the water cooler and was now staring into space and thinking grand moosian thoughts. The moose was a practical joke perpetrated by a sorcerer in the long-distant past. No one knew what the joke had been, who did it, or even whether it was funny or not. The spell that kept him alive was skillfully woven and surprisingly resilient. His joke complete, he had very little to do and most of eternity in which to do it, so he consequently looked painfully bored as he appeared and disappeared randomly about Zambini Towers. Although I'd spoken to him on many occasions, Hector had not replied—and since he was a large North American herbivore, I didn't really expect him to.

The Transient Moose stared at us both for a moment, gave a doleful sigh, and then faded from view.

"You didn't give that Phantom Twelve girl the ring, did you?" asked Tiger.

He knew me quite well by now. Despite being only twelve years old, he was pretty smart. Foundlings generally are.

"No—and I'm sorry you had to risk your neck because of it."

He shrugged and gave me a smile. "It was fun, actually. Except when I went down the well and got shot into the air. Do I tell the others we're five grand poorer because of you?"

"Better not."

I sifted through the mail for anything that looked desperately urgent—bills, mainly—and then checked the level of the background wizidrical radiation using a device called a shandargraph. Unlike the handheld shandarmeter, which measured local magical energy, the shandargraph gave an idea of broad trends of wizidrical energy over time—a bit like measuring atmospheric pressure. You could tell not only when a spell was being cast but how powerful it was and where.

I looked at the long ribbon of paper that was slowly emerging from the machine and noted that our morning's misadventure was dutifully recorded — fourteen megashandars, six miles away to the east. I could even see where it had peaked when Full Price tried to keep the well open. The spells undertaken by iMagic in Stroud were also apparent. Our workloads seemed relatively equal, although I knew for a fact that Blix would have the Truly Bizarre Tchango Muttney levitate a truck somewhere on the other side of town and hold it there for twenty minutes to make us *think* they had more work than they actually did.

iMagic was troublesome but not a real threat. With Blix, Tchango, and Dame Corby, She-Whom-the-Ants-Obey, iMagic had only three active sorcerers to our five. We also had two flying carpeteers and two decent precogs, of which they had none. But on the upside, they didn't have thirty-six barely sane ex-sorcerers to feed, and they also had a secondary income: Dame Corby was the heiress to the Corby Trouser Press empire, and yearly dividends were apparently still robust, despite the invention of drip-dry garments.

I picked up one of the two remaining self-cleaning cups from the drain rack and poured myself a tea from the never-ending teapot, then took some milk from the perpetually half-empty enchanted milk bottle in the fridge.

"Hello, Jennifer," said a voice from the sofa, and a very rumpled-looking figure sat up and scratched himself.

"Good morning, Kevin." I handed him a cup of tea and a cookie from the never-ending supply in the tin. "All well?"

Kevin was a lean man whose thirtieth birthday had passed unannounced two decades before. Despite his disheveled appearance in ratty clothes that would have been rejected by the most desperate Troll Wars Widow Fund thrift shop, he was clean-shaven and his finely cut hair was immaculate. He looked, in fact, like a businessman in a hobo costume.

"As well as ever," he replied with a yawn.

The reason Kevin always slept fully dressed on the office sofa when he had a perfectly good bedroom upstairs was because he had foreseen that he would die in his bed, and reasoned that if he stayed away from it, he wouldn't die. That might sound crazy until you consider that the Remarkable Kevin Zipp was one of our pre-cognitives, a breed of sorcerer that shuffled through millions of potential futures and occasionally picked out a winner. But as with all oracles, Kevin's visions could be vague and misleading. The time he foresaw "killer aliens from Mars" turned out to be "millers named Alan in cars," which isn't the same thing at all. And when he predicted the "reign of a matron named Grace," we actually got a "rain of meteors from space." Despite this, his strike rate was a respectable seventy-three percent and, since the Big Magic, improving still.

"Anything for us?" I asked. Quite often Kevin had dazzling visions that he never told anyone about, as he couldn't see their relevance.

"A few," he replied, taking a sip of tea. "Something about Vision Boss, and the price of elevators is set to fall."

"Fall?"

"Or rise. One of the two. Perhaps both."

"Vision Boss?" I asked, fetching the Visions Book, into which we logged every vision, notion, and foresight our pre-cognitives ever had. "You mean like the chain of eyeglass shops, 'Should have gone to Vision Boss'?"

"Not sure. It might have referred to the Boss of Visions — the greatest pre-cog ever."

"Sister Yolanda of Kilpeck has been dead more than twelve years," I said, writing Kevin's predictions in the Visions Book anyway. "Got hit by a tram on the High Road."

"Yes," said Kevin sadly, "didn't see that coming."

"Why would you be thinking of her?"

"I don't know. Oh, and I had another vision about the Great Zambini."

I was suddenly a lot more interested.

"You did?"

"He's going to reappear."

This was good news indeed. The Great Zambini had vanished eight months earlier while conducting a simple dematerialization during a children's party, and we'd been hoping to get him back ever since. Because Kevin and Mr. Zambini had known each other well, Kevin's predictions about Zambini's appearances were *always* correct—just too late for us to do anything useful with them.

"When?"

"Tomorrow afternoon at four-oh-three and fourteen seconds."

"Do you know where?"

"Not a clue—but he'll be there for several minutes."

"That's not so helpful," I pointed out. "There's an awful lot of *where* in the UnUK, and a minute isn't exactly much *when* in which to find him."

"Pre-cognition is not an exact science," grumbled Kevin defensively. "In fact, I don't think it's a science at all. But I may know more nearer the time."

"Can you predict when you might know?" I asked hopefully.

"No."

I allocated each vision a unique code—RAD094 to RAD096—in the Visions Book and then asked Kevin to tell me the second he knew more. The last time this happened, he'd had us all staking out a village in the weekends-only Duchy of Cotswold, where Mr. Zambini had reappeared for a full fifty-seven seconds before vanishing again. Despite fifteen of us dispersed around the village with eyes peeled, we missed Zambini, who turned up in a jam cupboard belonging to a Mrs. Bishop. He must have been confused about where he was, but not too confused; he managed to consume an entire jar of her best loganberry. And that was the problem with Zambini. He was rattling around the Now like a Ping-Pong ball, doing pretty much the same as the Transient Moose but with much broader geography and shorter visits. Wizard Moobin thought that Zambini must have corrupted his vanishing spell as he disappeared, but we wouldn't know for sure until we got him back — if we ever did.

"As soon as you get an *inkling* of a location, let me know," I told him again, and after asking Tiger to fetch Kevin some breakfast and the daily papers, I went and stared at the work schedule for the next few days. Wednesday and Thursday were straightforward, but all of Friday had been kept clear for the bridge job.

There was only one interesting bridge to speak of in Hereford, and that was the twelfth-century stone arched bridge. Or rather, that *had* been the most interesting bridge until the structure, weakened by neglect and heavy winter floods, collapsed three years before. It was now a pile of damp rubble, with only the remains of piers and abutments to indicate what had once been there.

"We need to rebuild the bridge without any hiccups, don't we?" said Tiger, noticing that I was staring at old photographs of the bridge.

"Yes, indeed," I replied. "Moving out of home improvements and into civil engineering projects could put Kazam firmly on the map. It'll be a good PR exercise, and we need to increase our standing within the community. I just hope Moobin knows what he's doing. He says he's got the rebuild planned, but I think his definition of *plan* might be more along the lines of 'make it up as we go along.'"

Tiger snapped his fingers. "Didn't Full Price say Moobin wanted us to witness an experiment he'd got cooking?"

"He did. Better go and see when he wants us. When you get back you can fill out the B1-7G forms for this morning's work—but not Perkins's involvement, remember."

He nodded and trotted out the door. A few minutes later I heard him yell as he fell up the elevator shaft, as was our way at Zambini Towers.

There was a knock at the office door and I turned to see a small man in a sharp suit, holding a briefcase. He looked vaguely familiar.

"My name is Mr. Trimble," announced the man, "of Trimble, Trimble, Trimble, Trimble, and Trimble, attorneys-at-law." He handed me a business card as his hat made its way automatically to the hat stand, part of a self-tidying spell that ran through the building.

"We've met before," I said coldly. "When you were representing the ConStuff Land Development Corporation."

"That was one of the *other* Trimbles," he said helpfully. "That's me there." He pointed to the second Trimble in the list on his card. "Donald was disbarred — a most unsavory episode."

"I see," I replied. "My name is Jennifer Strange, acting general manager of Kazam. Would you like a seat?"

Mr. Trimble took the proffered chair and got straight to the point. "I have wealthy and influential clients," he said, "and they have a proposal for Kazam."

I didn't like the sound of this, but at least Trimble was being honest — and I had five thousand moolah to earn back.

"Oh, yes?" I replied suspiciously. "What sort of proposal?"

Mr. Trimble took a deep breath. "My clients would like Kazam to reanimate the mobile telephone network."

It wasn't the first time we had been asked to switch the network back on, and it wouldn't be the last. Mobile phones had been one of the first devices to go when the drop in wizidrical power required the slow switch-off of services that ran, essentially, on magic. Mobile phones and computers hadn't been possible since 1993, color televisions since 1999, and GPS navigation since 2001. The last electromagical device to be switched off was the microwave oven in 2004, and that was only because aircraft radar used the same electromagical principle. The only magical technologies still running were north-pointing directional compasses and the spell that kept bicycles from falling over—both of which were so old that no one knew how to switch them off anyway.

"We've been approached by BellShout, N&O, and VodaBunny about this before," I said, "and our answer is the same: All in good time. The mobile phone network will be active just as soon as we have enough magic to bring back those electromagical technologies that have priority—medical scanners and then microwave ovens."

"Will that take long?"

I shrugged. "A while. When the electromagical spells were shut down, no one kept a hard copy of the spell. Much has to be rewritten. When you consider that a yo-yo has more than two hundred lines of spelltext to make it work and a photocopier more than ten thousand, you get an idea of the task. Besides, the switch-off gave us an opportunity to reconsider the direction magic will take. We can't make the same mistakes. Licensing the power of magic to individuals and companies placed sorcery in the hands of the unscrupulous. It has to be in the hands of all or none."

This was a view that the Great Zambini had embraced, and was shared by almost everyone at Kazam. Mr. Trimble and I stared at each other for a few moments.

"Well," he said, "would you take it to your sorcerers anyway? I'd like to report back to my clients that the refusal was unanimous."

I agreed I would speak to them, and Mr. Trimble rose to fetch his hat from the hat stand.

"I'm most grateful to you for your time," he said. "My clients will be very happy to talk if you change your position." And after shaking my hand, he left.

I wasn't alone for long. The prince dropped by with his day's schedule, and he wasn't happy.

"Pizza deliveries *again?*" he said in exasperation. "When do we do some proper carpeteering?"

"Maybe sooner than you think," I told him. "I've got a task for you."

His Royal Highness Prince Omar Smith Arkwright Ben Nasil was one of our carpeteers, which might have been a noble and exciting profession were it not for an incident one wintry night when the Turkmen Mk18C Bukhara on which Brother Velobius was carrying two passengers broke up in midair due to rug fatigue, killing all three riders. For safety reasons, the Civil Aviation Authority had introduced strict rules that made it almost impossible to turn a profit on magic carpet flight. Limited top speed, navigation lights — and worst of all, a ban on passengers. All we could do were deliveries.

"Here's the thing," I said. "Kevin Zipp has foretold the Great Zambini returning tomorrow afternoon at four-oh-three and fourteen seconds."

"Let me guess," said the Prince. "Kevin knows when but not where?"

"That's about the tune of it. We need Mr. Zambini back, Nasil, so stick to Zipp like a limpet. If he has a vision about where Zambini might show up, I want you to come and find me immediately."

Prince Nasil said he wouldn't fail me, made some comment about needing to take his carpet off the flight line next month for some remedial patchwork, and we said goodbye.

"Is he really a prince?" asked Tiger, who had just returned.

"Second in line to the Duchy of Portland," I told him. "What's the deal with Moobin?"

"He said come up anytime. He said you'd be impressed."

This worried me. Wizard Moobin liked a challenge, and was quite used to risking life and limb on weird experimental stuff that he described as important and cutting edge but I saw more as a nuisance.

"Let's do it." I sighed. "It's not like things could get more weird this morning."

SIX

Wizard Moobin

We walked toward the elevators.

"I hope he doesn't blow himself up again," I said.

"Or make himself attractive to badgers," added Tiger, reminding us of the time a badger-repellent spell had gone badly wrong and Zambini Towers had been inundated with winsome, lovelorn, black-and-white mustelids. Explosions and badger attraction aside, Moobin was easily our favorite sorcerer, as he was probably the most normal. He was in his mid-forties but looked a lot younger, and although more powerful than Lady Mawgon, he lacked precise control and often surged — which meant a sudden burst of wizidrical energy just when you didn't want it. Just before the Big Magic he had nearly blown us all to pieces when he turned lead into gold, and then blew up another laboratory while trying to invent a spell that reversed the effects of laboratories blowing up.

We took the elevator to the third floor by simply calling out the floor number and then stepping into the empty shaft. You fell to the floor you requested and had to step quickly out before you fell back down again. Unskilled users had been known to get stuck for some time, oscillating — on one occasion, for three days.

We found Moobin in his room, which was actually three rooms in one. He used it for both sleeping and tinkering, which explained the vast amount of apparatus lying about, none of which I understood but all of which looked dangerously complicated and hastily mended.

"Jennifer!" he remarked excitedly when he saw me. "How did the finding job go this morning?"

"It depends on your viewpoint. Did you hear that the Amazing Blix is attempting to accolade himself 'the All Powerful'?"

Moobin laughed. "His arrogance will be his undoing. Right, then," he continued, clapping his hands together. "To work. What's the Holy Grail of the Mystical Arts?"

I never saw Moobin so excited as when he was experimenting, and excitement made his wild hair look wilder and his unkempt style of dress shabbier. He looked less like a person, in fact, and more like an unmade bed with arms and legs.

"Invisibility?" I asked, incredulous, for not even the Mighty Shandar had ever achieved that. As far as we knew, no one had, although entire lives had been spent in the attempt.

"Okay," said Moobin, "what's the slightly-less-than-Holy Grail?"

"Moving cathedrals?" suggested Tiger.

"That's levitation," sniffed Moobin, "nothing more."

"Flying without a carpet or airplane under you?" I asked.

"Okay, even-*slightly*-less-than-Holy Grail?"

"Teleportation?" I said.

"*Exactly!*" replied Moobin excitedly. "The physical shifting from one place to another more or less simultaneously. The current record stands at eighty-five miles."

"The Great Zambini in his youth," I said to Tiger, "more than sixty years ago."

"My personal best," announced Moobin grandly, "is thirty-eight feet, and I'm going to try and increase that to . . . seventy."

"I see," I said, wondering what could go wrong and thinking of eight possibilities, ranging from the destruction of two city blocks to liquefying the earwax of those in the immediate vicinity — the usual domino effect of a teleportation. In fact, the purpose of the original enchantment had been *precisely* that: ear cleaning. Spooky instantaneous transportation was simply found to be a useful side effect. The wizard who wrote the original spell in 1698 had been beta-testing it as "an Improved and Much More Sanitary Method of Ear Cleansing" when he found himself inexplicably on the street outside. Much research followed and the range and accuracy of teleportation greatly increased, but the earwax issue had remained. You could always hear better at the end of a jaunt than at the beginning.

"Not only will I teleport seventy feet," continued Moobin dramatically, "but I will also travel though a sheet of three-millimeter plywood on the way."

Tiger and I looked at each other doubtfully. Moobin's last attempt to pass through solid objects had ended with a broken nose and a bruised knee.

"I've been working with silk, paper, and cardboard," he said as he led us into the corridor, "and it's time to move on up."

"And you're no longer leaving your clothes behind?" I asked, referring to an earlier and mildly embarrassing episode.

"Not at all," said Moobin, who hadn't been the one embarrassed. "I had been eating nougat earlier — I should have known better."

Due to its ex-hotel status, Zambini Towers was not

short on long corridors, and in the one outside his room, Moobin had hung a large sheet of plywood from a light fixture. He drew a cross on the floor about two yards in front of the wood, handed Tiger a pocket shandarmeter to measure peak wizidrical output, then gave me a tape measure to hold.

"Call out when I get to seventy feet, will you?" And he walked off holding the other end of the tape measure, beyond the plywood.

"Can't he teleport *around* the wood?" asked Tiger.

"Curved teleporting is not possible," I told him. "Magic's effect only works in straight lines. A teleportation around a corner means taking the shortest route *through* whatever the corner is made of. Passing through the rock and soil of the planet on a straight-line journey from here to Singapore takes a lot of wizidrical energy — it makes carpet travel a lot more crackle efficient than transcontinental teleportation. There *was* an enchanter years ago who experimented with high-end clear-air teleportation. He started from Paris and reappeared two and a half thousand feet over Toulouse."

"That must have been unexpected."

"On the contrary, it was planned — but his parachute failed to open, and he fell screaming to his death in a very undignified manner. The power of magic began to wane soon after, and no one tried it again."

"I can recommend hay carts for soft landings," Tiger

replied thoughtfully. "Sorcery isn't really straightforward at all, is it?"

After two months at Kazam, Tiger was still trying to get his head around the limiting practicalities of magic. Most people thought you just waved your hands and *sim-sallah-bim,* but it was a lot more complex than that. Sorcery was not so much doing what you wanted to do but doing what you *could* do—or ingeniously finding a way around the physical limitations of the craft.

The tape measure continued to pay out, and when it had reached seventy feet I called out and Moobin stopped.

"Okay, here we go, then," came Moobin's confident voice from the other end of the corridor. "Seventy feet and through a three-millimeter sheet of plywood."

I nodded to Tiger, who had lifted the cover from one of the many Magiclysm alarms on the walls of the building. If Moobin's spell went squiffy, Tiger would press the red button and the sprinklers in the ceiling would spray water to quench any spells. Wednesday morning was traditionally the spell-test day, and many of the residents wore galoshes and raincoats indoors on that day, just in case.

We heard a few grunts from the darkness beyond the sheet of wood, then a pause while nothing happened. There was another pause, more grunts, and then nothing happened again. It was just when nothing was about to happen for the third time that there was a faint *pop* from the other end of the corridor as the air rushed in to fill the hole where Moobin wasn't. A half second later he reappeared in front of us, the air he had displaced hitting us as a faintly discernible shock wave.

"Ta-da!" said Moobin, staring at his feet directly above the white cross. "Seventy feet, and through a sheet of three-millimeter plywood. Tomorrow I'll try six-millimeter ply, then chipboard."

"Impressive. I'll mark it up in the records ledger tonight," I said.

"It's also a new personal best," continued Moobin excitedly, "and if those heathen scum over at iMagic aren't also doing teleport work, it makes me the best teleporter on the planet. Why are you both staring at me?"

"You look like you've been glazed." I put out a hand to touch him. "Like a doughnut."

Just then, the separate sheets of thin wood veneer that made up the plywood fell neatly into three thin and very flappy pieces.

"Oh dear," said Moobin. "I appear to have picked up the glue from the plywood as I passed through. How did that happen?"

He wasn't asking any of us, of course; he was simply confused. But that was what research and development were like. Full of semi-triumphs and perplexing unforeseen consequences like the whole violent hiccupping thing when conjuring up fire — or the propensity for fillings to fall out of bystanders' teeth when attempting to tease a rainstorm out of a cloud.

"The Transient Moose can teleport almost without thinking," muttered Moobin, faintly annoyed, "*and* go around corners."

"But he's a spell himself," observed Tiger helpfully, "and presumably has zero mass, so it must be easier."

"Probably," replied Moobin gloomily. "I wish he'd let me have a closer look."

Wizard Moobin had recently fired a few spell probes into the Transient Moose to discover just what particular enchantment was keeping him going. The probes had shown little except that the original sorcerer was possibly Greek and the moose was most likely running Mandrake Sentience Emulation Protocols, which didn't help, as nearly all spells that made something appear lifelike are run under Mandrake.

It wasn't just curiosity. The Mystical Arts were arcane, secretive, and, once a specific spell was discovered, rarely shared. Ancient wizards went to their graves with the really groovy stuff still locked inside their heads. Some wrote it down in big leather-bound books, but most didn't. It would be very valuable indeed to find out not only how the moose managed to live so long and teleport so effortlessly, but how he could do it on an average crackle consumption of only 172.8 shandars a day.

"I'm going to take a shower," said Moobin, "as long as someone hasn't already swiped the hot water."

"Oops," said Tiger.

"What, again?" asked Moobin.

"I was covered in mud."

"Have you been thinking about the bridge gig, Moobin?" I asked, changing the subject. I had yet to see a detailed plan or risk assessment.

"I'm working on it," he said, "although with the Dibble coils stuck on standby, we'll need all of us if we're to do it in a day."

"Lady Mawgon is going to try to get them back online this morning."

"The old bat's going to try and hack the Dibble?" replied Moobin with a smile. "Better her than me." He nodded thoughtfully.

Hacking into a well-cast spell was not for the faint-hearted. Wizards guarded their work jealously and would often leave traps for busybodies attempting to copy their work. Tiger and I watched as Moobin went back into his room, mumbling as his feet made sticky footprints on the oak flooring.

"Right, then," I said, checking my watch. "Time to see Lady Mawgon. Don't mention the fact that we took no payment for the finding gig."

SEVEN

Hacking the Dibble

W hat the heck are Dibble Storage Coils?" asked Tiger as we made our way back downstairs. He still had a good decade's worth of learning to do, and only two years in which to do it. With the Great Zambini gone, I had to teach him most of it, and some of the stuff I hadn't even learned myself.

"It's a spell designed by Charles Dibble the Extraordinary," I explained. "In the days when wizidrical power was falling, the Great Zambini looked at several ways to store what crackle there was. Dibble the Extraordinary wasn't so much a practicing sorcerer but one who wrote spells for those who were. He wrote the entire mobile phone network incantation for ElectroMagic, Inc., back in the forties and then committed his energies to wiz-idrical storage devices. He was long retired when Zam-bini had him build the coils. Simply put, they transform Zambini Towers into something like a huge rechargeable battery."

Tiger looked around, as if wondering how he could have missed something so important.

"Where are they?"

I waved my hand around the building at large.

"You can't see the coils. They're more like a con-stantly circulating field of negative wizidrical energy that can absorb, store, and then discharge vast amounts of crackle on command. The applications are endless, from boring holes in solid rock to making something from nothing. We have the capacity to hold four giga-shandars."

"And what could a gigashandar actually do?" asked Tiger.

"It's a million shandars, or if you prefer to use the older imperial measurements, about twenty-six cathedral miles, which is enough crackle to—"

"Move a cathedral twenty-six miles?"

"You learn quick. Yes, or move twenty-six cathedrals one mile each, or a medium-size church five hundred miles, or, if you like, take a wardrobe all the way to Mel-bourne."

"Would there be any point to that?"

"Not really."

"So a capacity of four gigashandars is enough to move one cathedral — hang on — fifty-two miles?"

"Pretty much, although moving cathedrals cross-border by magic would be a bureaucratic nightmare. The paperwork would swamp you before you'd even gotten as far as Monmouth."

Tiger went silent for a moment. "I'm sensing there's a reason why cathedral moving is not on our price list."

"You sense right. Dibble died while servicing this enchantment twenty-six years ago. He left it in standby mode and passthought protected, so what we have now is a very, very big battery and no charger. It didn't matter when there was so little crackle, because Kazam didn't have a hope of doing any big jobs. But now that the power of magic is on the rise, we really need the Dibble back online if we're to do any serious magic like digging canals or laying railroad track or building henges or something."

"I get that," said Tiger, "kind of. But don't you think they should be called Zargon Coils or Znorff Inverters or something cool rather than Dibble?"

"Isn't Dibble cool?"

"No, not really. It's more dorky."

"I suppose you're right," I replied, "but real life isn't like that. Dibble invented them, so Dibble they are."

We walked across the lobby and into the Palm

Court. In the heyday of the Majestic Hotel, this would have been an exotic indoor garden of tropical plants, tall palms, and limpid pools with lily pads and koi. Scattered around would have been small tables of gossiping nobility taking tea, waited upon by attentive servers.

No longer.

The room had not been used for entertaining or growing tropical plants for years, and many of the glass panes in the bell-shaped roof were either cracked or missing. Buckets were scattered around to catch water during rainstorms, and the marble floor was stained and uneven. In the center of the room was a large and very dry fountain.

Standing next to it was Lady Mawgon. She had changed out of her usual black crinoline and into an even blacker one, which showed she meant business. Her clothes were so black, in fact, that they created a dark Lady Mawgon–shaped hole in the world, and it could give you vertigo if you stared too long.

"You never thanked me for putting the hay cart under you, Prawns."

"I'm most grateful to you for not letting me fall to a painful death," said Tiger, knowing it was senseless to argue.

"Good manners cost nothing," she grumbled. "Did Miss Shard pay up?"

"The matter was concluded satisfactorily," I replied.

"Hmm. Now, you are here to witness my attempt to hack into the Dibbles. You will not approach me and you will not talk. Do you understand?"

Tiger and I weren't sure if that meant we weren't to speak our answer, so we played it safe and nodded vigorously.

"Good. Primarily I will try to get into the root directory of the spell's central core to reset the passthought. From there I will attempt to switch the coils back on. You should take notes as I talk my way through it. I shall permit you to wish me good luck."

"Good luck, ma'am," I said, taking out my notebook and a pencil.

She turned to an empty space in the room and raised her index fingers. After a pause, she drew her hands downward and out, much like a conductor beginning a symphony. A blue-filled tear appeared in the air, as though she'd unzipped the flap of a tent. She continued to move her hands as if conducting, and as she signaled to an imaginary percussion section, the randomly placed chairs in the room moved away from the tear and the chandeliers tinkled slightly.

Lady Mawgon made a few flourishes, as one might do to signal in the entire string section, then held one hand in the air as if sustaining a note from the bassoons as she peered closer into the rent. The tear had depth within, and colored lights flashed to and fro as Lady

Mawgon subtly moved her hands between the theoretical harp and kettledrums to probe the inner workings of the spell. It was an incantation of great complexity, and Tiger and I stared wide-eyed. Spellbound, in fact. I'd worked around spells for years but had never actually *seen* one.

"Hmm," said Lady Mawgon, speaking over her shoulder while signaling an imaginary cello section to play pianissimo. "The enchantment is standard Waseed on a RUNIX core. The secondary spells are off-the-rack Shandar to self-regulate the internal fields, but it seems Dibble added a few gatekeepers to thwart a hack, then set them orbiting the central core in all five directions at once so they couldn't be unwoven."

"The Great Zambini was always cautious," I replied, risking her anger by breaking my silence. "He thought four gigashandars of raw crackle lying around might tempt a fallen wizard with mischief on the mind. He wanted it protected."

"You might be right," said Lady Mawgon.

There followed about five minutes of hard spelling, almost indistinguishable from the gestures of a conductor. Mr. Zambini had told me that the skills are interchangeable, and that the myth about wands might have begun with a conductor's baton.

Tiger and I were just beginning to get bored and think of other things to do when our ears popped.

"Okay," Lady Mawgon said, giving a rare smile. "I'll just reset the passthought, and we're done."

She made a few more flourishes to an illusory wood-wind section, and the rent closed.

"There," she said triumphantly. "I'm surprised it was so easy. The coils will be full by this time tomorrow, and we can run a test spell with them by Friday morning in time for the bridge job. Prawns, go and fetch Moobin so I can share the passthought."

Tiger hurried out and I congratulated her on the work.

"I could have done it in my sleep ten years ago," she replied, "but I thank you for your praise. Why are you staring at me?"

"You're going gray," I said.

"I've been gray for years," she said, "and I've warned you against impertinence."

"No, no," I replied, "*everything* on you is going gray."

And so she was. Her black crinoline dress was now a charcoal color and lightening by the second. Lady Mawgon frowned, looked at her hands, then stared at me with a wan smile.

"Blast," she said in a resigned tone, and a few moments later she had turned entirely to stone.

"Oh, poo," I said quietly to myself.

EIGHT

Turned to Stone

I'd never seen anyone turned to stone before, and after the initial shock wore off, I ventured closer. Every single pore of Lady Mawgon's skin, every wrinkle, every eyelash, was perfectly rendered in the finest alabaster. It felt odd being in such close proximity to her even if she was now a four-hundred-pound block of stone, and although getting turned to stone was bad news, it might have been worse. The really serious cases of petrification involved dolerite, marble, or, worst, granite.

"Goodness," Moobin said with a laugh as he walked in, closely followed by Tiger, "the old girl will never hear the end of this. Dibble the Extraordinary lived up to his name—a stoning incantation as a gatekeeper. Well, well, never would have thought of it."

"Can you change her back?" I asked.

"Child's play. Although to be honest, it *is* a lot quieter with her like this."

"If I draw a mustache on her," added Tiger, "will she still have it when she changes back?"

"It's not funny," I said, even though I, too, had mixed feelings. "I'd be happier to have her back in one piece as soon as possible."

"Very well," said Moobin, and after taking a deep breath, he drew himself into the hard spelling posture, pointed both index fingers at her, and let fly.

Nothing happened.

He stood up, relaxed, then tried again.

Still nothing happened.

"That's odd," he said at last. "Did she change to stone quickly?"

"About five seconds."

"Oh dear. Wait here a moment." And he ran out the door.

"She still looks kind of frightening, doesn't she?" said Tiger.

She did, even though her features were trapped not in the usual Mawgon look of scowling displeasure but in the resigned smile she'd had when she realized that the long-dead Dibble had outwitted her.

"Still," said Tiger, "it proves what I always thought."

"What's that?"

"That she does wear roller skates under her dress."

I looked down, and just peeking out from the soft white folds of her gypsum prison was the shape of a roller skate wheel pressed against her hem.

"Holy cow!" said Half Price as he walked in, accompanied by Full Price and Wizard Moobin. "I've never seen her looking so *stony* before."

"She's certainly stuck between a rock and a hard place," added Full Price with a giggle. "Did you try the standard Magnaflux Reversal?"

"I tried it twice," said Moobin. "Not a flicker."

"Let me try," said Half, and let fly in a similar manner as Moobin, with similar results.

"Hmm," he said. "Full?"

His brother tried and failed also. The sorcerers suddenly looked a lot more serious and went into one of those wizidrical discussions where I generally understood one word in eight. After ten minutes of this, they all let fly together, but all that happened was that the room grew hot and clammy and our clothes became a size larger.

"Did she say anything before she went?" asked Moobin, tightening his belt a notch.

"Only that the coils were taking on power," I replied, "and that the spell was written in RUNIX."

"No one writes in RUNIX anymore," said Full Price.

"It's an archaic spell language that was big in the fourth century before we moved over to ARAMAIC. Half, who's our RUNIX expert?"

"Aside from Lady Mawgon?"

"Yes, obviously."

"Monty Vanguard always had an interest in old spell languages."

Moobin sent Tiger to fetch Vanguard. The atmosphere, which earlier had been a bit silly, was now deathly serious.

"But the Fundamental Spell Reversibility Rule still applies, doesn't it?" I asked.

"Totally," agreed Moobin. "There's no spell cast that can't be unraveled if you know precisely how it was written—it just may take a while to figure out."

"How long?" I asked.

"If we work through lunchtimes, about six to seven years."

"Years?" I echoed in some alarm. "The bridge gig starts on Friday. We've got less than forty-eight hours!"

"Life is short, magic is long, Jennifer."

"That's not helpful."

"Having a spot of bother?" asked a dapper white-haired man in impeccable dress and a thin mustache. This was Monty Vanguard, one of our spellers. Long in retirement, he spent his days putting together the thousands of lines of spell we would need to bring medical scanners back online someday.

Moobin explained the problem at length, and Monty Vanguard smiled.

"So you young blades have got your fingers burned and need an oldster to help you out, hmm?"

"Something like that."

Monty opened the rent in the air just as Mawgon had done and, after donning his glasses, looked around inside the enchantment.

"I get it," he said after a while. "Do we have the passthought?"

"No," I replied. "She turned to stone before she told anyone."

"I'll reset it. Are you sure we want Lady Mawgon back? I mean, she's —"

Monty Vanguard didn't finish his sentence — for he too turned to alabaster. Not slowly, like Mawgon, but instantly. It was his bad luck that he had been blinking at the time, so instead of looking elegant and dignified in stone, he had that annoying half-closed-eye look that makes one seem a bit, well, dopey.

"Okay," said Full Price after a pause. "That didn't turn out so well. What now?"

No one had any suggestions, so we stood there, staring at Monty and Lady Mawgon.

"Will it harm them?" I asked. "Being stone, I mean?"

"Not in the least," Moobin replied. "As long as we keep them away from a sandblaster and no one borrows part of them to mend the front portico of Hereford Cathedral, they'll not know even one second has passed."

And that was when I was struck by an idea that might explain something that had been confusing me for a while: how the Great Zambini and Mother Zenobia both managed to live longer than a century with only a small level of decrepitude. In Zenobia's case, it was well over a hundred and fifty years.

"Can I be excused?" I asked. "I've got an idea."

"Of course," replied Moobin, "but let's keep this top-secret. This is something only the five of us need know about."

"Six," said Tiger, for Transient Moose had suddenly appeared and was staring at Lady Mawgon with a detached interest.

"Six, then. No sense in panicking the residents, hmm?"

I quickly fetched some cardboard and a felt pen from the office and placed a sign outside the entrance of the Palm Court that read CLOSED FOR REDECORATION.

"What now?" asked Tiger as we walked through the lobby.

"We're going to visit Mother Zenobia."

He gave a shudder. "Do I have to come?"

"Yes."

"She frightens me."

"She frightens me, too. Think of it as character building. Go and find your tie, polish your shoes, and fetch the Youthful Perkins. The convent is in the same direction as the castle. We'll take Perkins to his magic license test afterward. I'll meet you both outside in ten minutes."

Quarkbeast and Zenobia

I kept my Volkswagen in the garages beneath Zambini Towers, where it shared a dusty existence with several dilapidated Rolls-Royces and a Bugatti or two, remnants of when the retired sorcerers had money and power. Aside from the Slayermobile, which was also kept there now that my recent role of Dragonslayer was over, mine was the only working car. Since the Kingdom of Snodd grant-ed licenses not by age but by who was mature enough to be put in charge of half a ton of speeding metal, no male under twenty-six or wizard ever possessed a driver's li-cense. Because of this I was compelled to add taxi service to my long list of jobs.

I pulled around to the front of the building, parked the car, and turned off the engine. Lady Mawgon's unfortunate accident might mean postponing the bridge gig, which I was loath to do; it would make Kazam look weak when we were trying to promote ourselves as strong and confident. Even if Perkins did get his license, we would still have only five wizards to rebuild the bridge—and we needed six to be sure.

I sighed and gazed absently across the street. On the opposite side of the road was the Quarkbeast memorial, Kazam's tribute to a loyal friend and ally who had given his life to protect me and had contributed in no small measure to the success of the Big Magic. I thought about him a lot, and although he had often frightened small children, he had been a steadfast companion until the end.

I frowned. There seemed to be a corner missing out of the oolitic limestone plinth upon which the statue sat. I got out of the car and walked across for a closer look.

I was right; something had gnawed a chunk out of the plinth. There was a broken tooth stuck in the stone, and I tugged until it came free. It was a sharp canine, colored the dull slate gray of tungsten carbide.

"What have you found?" Tiger had just come outside. He had also been fond of the Quarkbeast, even though he'd known it only a short time. He had often

been dragged around the park on the beast's early morning walks—but in an affectionate, non-malicious,
hardly-hurting-you-at-all sort of way.

"Look," I said, dropping the tooth into his palm. "It
looks like there's another Quarkbeast in town. That'll
have the town council in a lather—the Beastcatcher is
very pro-Quarkbeast and rarely favors extermination."
This annoyed the council, as they saw the role of the
Beastcatcher as very much like pest control. The previous Beastcatcher had been much more popular but sadly
got himself eaten by a Tralfamosaur who took offense at
being poked at with a stick.

"This beast might not be staying," said Tiger, staring at the tooth. "Just paying its respects on its way
through."

I held a special affinity for the Quarkbeast, a small
hyena-shaped creature covered in shiny leathery scales
and often described as one-tenth Labrador, six-tenths
Velociraptor, and three-tenths kitchen food blender. Not
just because I owed my life to one, but because they were
one of the Ununited Kingdoms' surviving eight species
of invented animals, all created by notable wizards starting in the sixteenth century, when enchanted beasts were
totally the thing. The Mighty Shandar had created the
Quarkbeast for a bet in 1783 and apparently won the
wager, as nothing more bizarre has ever been created.

That didn't stop them from being uniquely dangerous, and a Quarkbeast was regarded with a great deal of suspicion by the authorities—hence the issue with the Beast-catcher. An abiding fondness for metal is one of its many peculiar habits, zinc most of all. In fact, the first sign of a Quarkbeast in the neighborhood is that the shiny zinc coatings are licked off the trash cans, the beast equivalent of licking the icing off a cake.

I looked around cautiously, hoping to catch a glimpse of the small creature. There was no sign, so we walked back to the car.

"Do you think this Quarkbeast could have been the other half of your pair, all the way from Australia?" asked Tiger, fastening his seat belt.

"Quarkbeasts come in pairs?" asked Perkins, who had buckled himself into the back seat. Although quite expert in seeding ideas, he was not so hot when it came to magicozoology.

"They don't so much breed as replicate," I explained. "They divide into two entirely equal and mirror-opposite Quarkbeasts. But as soon as they do, they have to be separated and sent a long way from each other—opposite sides of the globe, usually. If a paired positive and negative Quarkbeast meet, they are both annihilated in a flash of pure energy. It was said that Cambrianopolis was half destroyed when a confluence of paired Quarkbeasts came together and exploded with the force of ten thousand tons of Marzex-4. Luckily, Cambrianopolis is such a ruin, no one really noticed."

"I heard it was an earthquake," said Perkins.

"That's usually the cover story. We can't have people panicking like idiots as soon as they see a Quarkbeast. The general population is suspicious enough of magic as it is."

"I suppose not."

"Why do Quarkbeasts search for their twin?" asked Tiger.

"I don't know," I replied. "Boredom?"

"If it's the match of *your* Quarkbeast," said Perkins with growing confusion, "doesn't that mean the new Quarkbeast is unlikely to explode? It can't ever find its pair."

"Exactly. Nothing to fear from this one."

We drove off in silence, past the cathedral and out of the city walls, then headed south into the Golden Valley. We passed Snodd Hill and the castle, with the Dragonlands beyond, and went down the escarpment to the small town of Clifford. There, on a bend in the river and set about with oak and sweet chestnut, was the place Tiger and I had called home for the first twelve years of our lives. It was as grim as we both remembered it, and Tiger and I glanced at each other as we drew up outside. Perkins took one look at the Convent of the Blessed Ladies of the Lobster and announced he would be staying in the car.

"It's not that bad," said Tiger defensively. "The foundlings rarely have to share blankets these days, and gruel no longer has a consistency thinner than water."

"I wonder how they did that," I mused, since gruel's primary ingredient *is* water. "I've always wanted to know."

"It must be hard to extract the nourishment out of water," agreed Tiger, "but they managed it somehow."

"I'll leave you both to your trip down memory lane," said Perkins, staying resolutely in the back seat and hover-orbiting a pair of snooker balls around each other as a tuning-up exercise for his magic test. "I'll see you guys later."

We walked across the parking lot, up to the great doors, past the slot in the door for after-hours foundling deliveries, and into the quadrangle. I felt Tiger clasp my hand.

"It's okay," I said. "No one's taking you back. We're owned by Kazam now. Everything's fine."

We walked across the quad, where open-air lessons were held in the summer and from where we used to watch shells lobbed across the border from King Snodd's artillery battery into the small Duchy of Brecon across the river. Although the guns were now silent and an uneasy peace had descended between Brecon and Snodd, we had driven past a squadron of landships on our way in. The six-story-high tracked vehicles had no special significance to me, but they did to Tiger, although he didn't know it — Mother Zenobia had told me that Tiger's parents had been a husband-and-wife engineering team on a landship that vanished during the Fourth Troll War. Tiger would have been lost, too, had childcare facilities not been removed from the landships in order to make room for extra munitions. When his parents never returned he ended up on the steps of the orphanage.

Mothers and fathers are a touchy subject for foundlings, which was why Tiger had not yet been told what happened. The whole abandonment deal could devour you, so we foundlings usually left it alone until we felt we had the maturity to deal with it. My own parents would probably be traceable through my Volkswagen, as I had been left on the front seat; although I was probably mature enough to handle knowing more, life was complicated enough.

"Is that Jennifer?" said Mother Zenobia as we were shown into her office. "I can smell early Volkswagen upon you. A mix of burned oil, hot mud, and six-volt electrics."

"It is, ma'am."

"And those footsteps behind you. Guarded and impertinent — yet full of inner strength to be later realized. Master Prawns?"

"Your servant, ma'am," said Tiger.

Mother Zenobia was not only old but completely blind, and had been since before most people on the planet were born. She was sitting in an armchair in front of a fire, her gnarled fingers resting on the top of her cane. Her face was so suffused with wrinkles that lost baby tortoises often followed her home. She clapped her hands and a novice entered, took orders for tea or cocoa, bobbed politely, and then left again.

"So," said Mother Zenobia after offering us a seat each, "is this a social visit or business?"

"Both," I said, "and please excuse my impertinence, Mother Zenobia, but our conversation must be strictly in confidence."

"May my ears be infested by the floon beetle if I murmur so much as a word, Jennifer. Now, what's up?"

"Lady Mawgon got herself changed to stone."

A smile crossed Mother Zenobia's features. "Silly Daphne. What was she trying to do?"

I explained about the storage coils and what had transpired.

"Not like Mawgon to get caught out by a gate-keeper," murmured Mother Zenobia. "What is this to do with me? My sorcery days are long over." She held up her hands as if we needed proof. They were twisted with arthritis, her valuable index fingers bent and, for a sorcerer, almost useless.

I chose my words carefully. Moobin had said earlier that getting changed to stone was effectively suspended animation.

"I thought perhaps great age in sorcerers might be less about spelling away old age and more like pressing the Pause button."

"You are a highly perceptive young lady," replied Zenobia. "I do indeed change to stone every night in order to delay death's cold embrace. Eight hours of sleep over an eighty-year lifetime is about twenty-six years. Wasted time, if you ask me, except for dreaming, which I miss. I've been rock during the winter months for the past seventy-six years as well, and when my last fortnight beckons I will be with you for an hour a year. I may last another century at this rate."

She thought for a moment.

"Self-induced petrification has its drawbacks, though. Changing to limestone at night is no problem, but returning to life in the morning leaves minute traces of calcite in the fine capillaries of the retina."

Tiger and I looked at each other. The secret of Mother Zenobia's longevity was no more.

"You won't tell anyone, will you?" she added. "It's all strictly prohibited by the *Codex Magicalis* under 'enchantment abuse.'"

"Your secret is safe with us," I assured her. "So this is

how the Great Zambini looks seventy when he is actually one hundred and twelve?"

"Indeed," replied Mother Zenobia, as the novice returned with the tea and cocoa, bobbed politely, and then went out again. "But he can do it better than I. He turns to dolerite and thus has none of the sight difficulties I have with limestone. The really class acts turn themselves to granite, which has no side effects at all."

"The Mighty Shandar," I breathed, suddenly realizing that he, too, must change himself to stone on a regular basis. "That would explain how he has lived for almost five centuries."

"Right again," said Zenobia. "It is said that his dynastic family of agents have instructions to only wake him for the best jobs. They say that the Mighty Shandar won't get out of black granite for less than eight drayweights of gold a day, and that he has not lived longer than a minute since 1783, the year he finished the Channel Tunnel."

"He could live almost forever," I observed.

"In *theory* one might," said Mother Zenobia. "Using petrification to suspend animation indefinitely is less dependent on the spell and more a case of not letting things drop off. Pity those wizards from ancient Greece missing their arms, legs, or heads. Come out of a two-millennium sleep missing an arm, and you'd bleed to death within five minutes. Still, most of them would have been enchanted in RUNIX, and you wouldn't know how to release them anyway."

"Which brings me back to why we are here," I said. "The spell gatekeeper of which Lady Mawgon fell afoul was written in RUNIX, and we wanted to know how you might reverse that, given your expertise in these matters."

"My spell is written in ARAMAIC-128," she said, shaking her head, "which allows for perfectly timed depetrification. You need to find someone who is expert in RUNIX. What about the Great Zambini?"

This suggestion offered at least a possibility. I told Mother Zenobia about Mr. Zambini's possible appearance the next day, and she nodded sagely.

"I hope it works out. Bored now. Go away. Drink your cocoa."

So we did, and since it was quite hot and we felt we should leave soon, we drank a little more quickly than was good for us, and it made our eyes water. We left Mother Zenobia soon after and, with burned tongues, walked back toward the car. I now knew how Zenobia, Shandar, and Zambini had lived for so long, but it wouldn't really help us turn Lady Mawgon back.

"We *really* need to find the Great Zambini this time," I said.

"Is it likely?" asked Tiger, who had been on several Zambini searches and knew the pitfalls.

"If past attempts are anything to go by, we have two chances: fat and slim."

We walked outside and found Perkins peacefully asleep in the back seat, the paint of the once orange Beetle slowly turning from blue to green to black and then back to blue again. He was ready.

The King's Useless Brother

We partly retraced our route back toward Hereford, but instead of going straight ahead by the grave of the unknown tattooist at Dorstonville, we took the four-lane processional avenue that led toward the king's modest eight-story palace at Snodd Hill. The castle covered six square acres, with many of the kingdom's administrative departments scattered among its two hundred or so rooms. A roof of purple slate topped the stone building, and the eighteen towers were capped with smaller, conical towers, each home to a long pennant that fluttered elegantly in the breeze.

After making our way through three drawbridges,

each with its own peculiar brand of pointless and over-long security procedures, we eventually made it to the inner bailey, where we parked the car outside the Interior Ministry. I told Tiger to wait for us there, and I walked Perkins to the correct desk. I came in here quite a lot, usually to submit the endless forms and paperwork that bedeviled modern sorcery.

"Hello, Miss Strange," said the receptionist. "Here to submit more paperwork?"

"Magic license," I replied, nodding toward Perkins. "We have an appointment to see the King's Useless Brother."

She stared at us both over her spectacles for a moment, consulted the schedule, and then pointed us toward the uncomfortable bench. The one with cushions was reserved for those of higher birth and was today crammed with bewigged aristocracy who, by their refusal to sit on the citizens' bench, made themselves doubly uncomfortable.

Perkins and I talked through the application process. I was more nervous than I thought I'd be, probably because we were one sorcerer down for the foreseeable future, and Perkins was going to have to prove himself pretty fast if we still wanted to do the bridge gig on Friday.

"How do you think I'm going to do?" he asked.

"You'll pass or my name's not Jennifer Strange."

"Your name's not Jennifer Strange."

"What?"

"You're a foundling. You don't know what your name is."

"It *could* be Jennifer Strange," I said unconvincingly, "as a sort of coincidence."

"It doesn't seem very likely."

"Perhaps not. But listen, you're going to pass, right?" And I took his hand, squeezed it, and smiled at him, and he smiled back.

"Thanks."

"Miss Strange?" said the receptionist. "The King's Useless Brother has become bored and will see you early."

Perkins and I straightened our clothes and followed her into a high-ceilinged room decorated in the "medieval dreary chic" style that was very much in fashion: a lot of stone, tapestries on the walls, and a stylish cold draft that caught you in the small of the neck like the onset of pneumonia.

Sitting behind a large desk full of shiny executive desk toys was the King's Useless Brother, a thin, weedy man with a constantly dripping nose that he dabbed with annoying regularity on a handkerchief.

"Good afternoon, Your Gracious Uselessness," I said, bowing low. "I am Jennifer Strange of the Kazam House of Enchantment. I humbly beg to set before you an application for my client, Mr. Perkins Archibald Perkins, to be licensed to commit enchantments in the worthy Kingdom of Snodd."

"Eh?" he said, so I said the same thing again, only this time much more slowly. When I had finished, he thought for a moment and then said, "You want a magic license?"

"Yes."

"Then why didn't you just say so? All that 'gracious this' and 'humbly beg' makes my head spin. I wish people would say what they want rather than hiding it in long words. Honestly, if we got rid of any word longer than eight letters, life would be a lot more understandable."

"Except you wouldn't have been able to say 'understandable,'" pointed out Perkins.

The King's Useless Brother thought carefully and counted on his fingers.

"How right you are!" he announced at length. "What were we talking about?"

"A magic license application?" I prompted.

"Of course. But tell me one thing before we look at the application."

"Yes?" I asked, expecting to be quizzed about Perkins's fitness to serve, whether he would uphold the noble calling with every atom of his being, that sort of thing.

"How can you be called Perkins Perkins?"

"My father's name was Perkins, and I'm named after him. It's like Adam Adams or David Davies."

"Or William Williams," I added.

"Who's he?"

"Someone I just made up."

"Oh," said the Useless Brother, sniffing. "Right. What happens now?"

I took a deep breath. "I explain exactly why Mr. Perkins should receive a license, and upon your approval, we turn to appendix F of the Magic Enactments Licensing Act of 1867 and conduct one spell each from Group A through to Group G. Afterward, once opposition voices are heard, Mr. Perkins performs his Great Feat. You then decide upon the merits of the case and stamp the application into authority . . . or not."

"Stamp?" His attention, which had been drifting somewhat, was suddenly renewed. "I have a number of stamps for all different purposes — look."

He jumped off his chair and opened a cupboard behind the desk. It was full of rubber stamps: big ones, small ones, each elegantly made and presumably designed to enact some sort of legislation for which the Useless Brother had been made responsible.

"This is the one we will use today," he said, selecting an ornately handled rubber stamp the size of a grapefruit. "It carries two colors on a single stamp, which is a remarkable achievement, don't you think? Now, where do I stamp it?"

Perkins and I looked at each other. This was turning out to be much easier than we had thought.

"Don't you want to see Cadet Perkins perform his Great Feat, at the very least?" I asked. "Or even have the adjudicator present?"

"Oh, I'm sure he'll be fine," said the King's Useless Brother dismissively, staring at the stamp lovingly. I shrugged. The stamp made it all legal, and we'd be fools to pass up such an easy opportunity.

"Just here," I said, passing the application across the desk.

"This is the part I like," he said excitedly. "There's nothing quite like the satisfying *thump* of a rubber stamp on paper. The sound of freedom, don't you think?"

He opened a jewel-encrusted pad, reverentially inked the stamp, brought it up above his head, paused for a moment, and —

"One moment, sire."

Two men had just walked in. The most important of them was Lord Tenbury, the king's most trusted advisor and the King's Useless Brother's business partner. He was a man dressed in the robes of high office, with a finely combed gray beard and hair that framed his piercing eyes, also gray. I had met him on a number of occasions, and he always left me with the impression that he was an iron fist in a kid-leather glove. Pleasant on the surface, but too smart and savvy to let much get past him. He was loyal to the crown through and through — and not averse to making a few sacks of cash on the side.

The other man was Conrad Blix, chief wizard and general manager of iMagic.

What was *he* doing here?

"My gracious lord!" exclaimed Tenbury in an exasperated tone. "What did we say about stamping things when I'm out of the room?"

"Sorry," said the Useless Brother, looking bored, "but she seemed so nice, and that person there has the same first name as his last name."

"Perkins," said Perkins helpfully.

"I see," said Tenbury, looking at us both suspiciously. "And why are you here before your allotted time?"

"We were invited in," I said.

"That's true," said the Useless Brother. "It gets very lonely in here sometimes with no stamping to do."

"You could always look out the window."

"Of course I can't, *silly*," scolded the Useless Brother. "If I did that all morning, I'd have nothing to do in the afternoon."

"Very well," said Tenbury with a sigh. "Have we seen the mandatory magic demonstrations or heard opposition statements?"

The Useless Brother frowned. "Opposition . . . what?"

"Have we?" asked Tenbury, looking at me.

"No, sir, although we did ask. His Uselessness waived the normal procedure —"

"Then I must with all haste *reinstate* it," interrupted Tenbury. "I am sure you appreciate the importance of protocol and procedure, not to mention the possibility of falling afoul of King Snodd's No Hoodwinking of Simpletons Law, specifically enacted for his brother?"

"My apologies, sir," I said, bowing low. "I meant no disrespect."

Tenbury smiled, and did so with considerable charm. It would be easy to trust him, and that would be one's first and last mistake. Unlike King Snodd and his mediocre dignitaries with their false charm, Tenbury was actually quite good at it. I could imagine him saying, "Terribly sorry about this, old boy," as he put someone on the torture rack.

"But first," he continued, "pleasantries. Good afternoon, Miss Strange."

I bobbed politely. "Good afternoon, Your Grace. May I present Cadet Perkins Perkins, here to apply for a license to perform magic? Cadet Perkins, this is Lord Tenbury, the king's chief advisor."

"Good afternoon," said Tenbury with a smile,

shaking Perkins's hand. "So good of you to come. I expect you know this much-respected citizen?"

He indicated the man who had walked in with him: Conrad Blix. As usual, Blix was dressed all in black — not the long, flowing gowns of old wizidrical tradition but a sharply tailored suit complete with black shirt, black tie, black socks, black shoes, and, if the rumors were correct, black underwear. He was a lean man in his early fifties with graying hair dyed black, a carefully coiffured goatee, and upswept eyebrows that he had trained to work independently of each other for increased dramatic effect. He also had the annoying habit of keeping his chin high, so he appeared — if you were shorter, which most people were — to be looking down his nose at you.

Blix and I looked at each other coldly. The disdain I felt wasn't just me; it was universal. Blix thought it was because his grandfather had been the much-hated Blix the Hideously Barbarous and everyone was needlessly prejudiced over the power-mad descendant, but the truth was more plain: He just wasn't very likable.

"Have trouble with a spell this morning?" he asked.

I hoped my consternation didn't show. "What makes you say that?"

"Several blips on the shandargraph that were centered on Zambini Towers," he said. "One large dip at eleven fifteen that you had kindly warned me about, several more ten minutes later, a pause, and then a massive drain that almost flatlined the trace. It looked suspiciously like somebody got into trouble, and another tried to reverse it. They failed and then everyone tried together. Yes?"

He was entirely correct.

"Not at all," I replied. "We were simply limbering up for the bridge gig on Friday. There'll be some heavy lifting to do, and Patrick of Ludlow can't be expected to shoulder all the work on his own."

I could see Blix didn't believe me, but I had other things on my mind. Not least, why was Blix buddying up with Lord Tenbury? I smelled a rat, and suspected it would not be long in making an appearance.

"We haven't met," said Blix to Perkins, so I apologized and introduced them.

"I humble myself in your presence, sire," said Perkins politely, for irrespective of how you viewed him, Blix was still a skilled practitioner. "I saw you a few years back, levijuggling thirty-two billiard balls, each in an entirely separate orbit and at its own speed. It was quite something."

"Too kind," replied Blix with a bow.

"That's enough preamble," said Lord Tenbury. "With His Eminence Ruprecht Sawduzt Snodd's approval, we should look at Mr. Perkins's application."

"Who?" asked Blix and I almost at the same time. Tenbury pointed at the King's Useless Brother, who was doodling absently on his desk blotter.

Lord Tenbury pressed a button on the intercom and asked for Miss Smith to be sent in. I saw Blix stiffen when Tenbury mentioned her name, and I felt my pulse quicken, too. The door opened and an upright woman in early middle age with a shock of white hair walked in. Her eyes were so dark they seemed empty, and an undefinable damp silence like that in caves moved in with her.

"Thank you — um — for joining us, Miss Smith," said Tenbury, shivering as he spoke.

"Right," she replied, her dark eyes glaring at Blix so savagely that I saw the color drain from his cheeks.

This was Miss Boolean Smith, once known as the Magnificent Boo. She'd been a powerful independent sorceress of considerable talents until she was kidnapped by anti-magic extremists. She had never practiced again following her release, nor revealed why. The only time she did anything related to magic was in her usual job as Beastmaster.

Today she was obviously serving as the Infernal Affairs–nominated adjudicator, to ensure that no trickery influenced Perkins's practical demonstrations. It would be simplicity itself to have another wizard outside doing spells on Perkins's account, or even a disgruntled wizard attempting to thwart Perkins with a jam, and Boo was there to detect any chicanery.

"It is a great pleasure to meet you again," I said, since we had spoken occasionally on the subject of Quark-beasts, about which she was an expert. "May I present Cadet Perkins?"

The Once Magnificent Boo glared at Cadet Perkins but did not shake his outstretched hand. She never shook hands — not with anyone.

"I am much honored," said Perkins, trying to avoid her jet-black eyes.

"Then you honor too easily," she replied before turning to Blix. "Still drowning puppies, Conrad?"

"That was never proven," replied Blix as the temperature in the room lowered another two degrees.

"Pleasantries are over," said Tenbury nervously. "The paperwork, if you please, Miss Strange."

I presented the paperwork to the King's Useless Brother, who stared at it absently for a few seconds before Tenbury checked it and then passed it to Once Magnificent Boo, who grunted her approval.

"You may proceed," said Tenbury.

"This is my chosen spell from Group A," announced Perkins, as the King's Useless Brother and the chair he was sitting in elevated several feet, rotated once slowly, and were then set back down again.

"Gosh," said the Useless Brother.

"Accepted," said Boo.

Over the next twenty minutes, Perkins undertook several other acts of enchantment, which by their variety and scope demonstrated his understanding of the Mystical Arts. He turned water in a jug blue, made a light bulb glow without wires, and took off his own undershirt without removing his shirt, which sounds easy but is actually one of the hardest to do in Group C. In fact, he managed all the tasks without a problem and to Boo's approval, and after several more assorted enchantments we were ready to hear any opposition arguments.

This is where I expected Blix to drum up some technicality, perhaps in retaliation for our observation that iMagic's Samantha Flynt had been less than perfect in her magic feats, and that conducting her test in a swimsuit was pointless and demeaning to the profession and women in general. He could have tried to block us, but he didn't.

"We have no objections to Mr. Perkins's application," he said.

This was suspicious — mostly because that's what any reasonable person might have said, and Blix was rarely, if ever, reasonable.

Perkins was now ready to undertake his last act of sorcery, which was to be a class-six enchantment of one's own invention that "must show originality and flair, and be between one and three thousand shandars."

"For my final enchantment," declared Perkins, "I will set distant dogs barking."

"What?" said the King's Useless Brother. "That's it? This is *most* unsatisfactory. I was hoping for a shower of mice or conjuring up a marshmallow the size of my head or something."

"It does sound a bit . . . easy," added Lord Tenbury.

"I concur that it *sounds* lame," said Perkins, "but making distant dogs bark is a spell of considerable subtlety that combines distance, canine mind control, and pinpoint selectivity."

"Cadet Perkins is correct," said Once Magnificent Boo quietly. "The test is valid."

"Very well," said Lord Tenbury. "Proceed."

"Yes," said the Useless Brother. "Proceed."

We stepped onto the ramparts outside the Infernal Affairs office, a section of flat lead roof on the high outer wall of the castle. Eight stories below us was the courtyard, and from our lofty perch we could see the Dragonlands, a vast tract of unspoiled land, untrod by humans for more than four centuries and now home to the only two dragons on the planet, Feldspar Axiom Firebreath IV and Colin.

"Ladies and gentlemen," began Perkins, "for this test

I will set four distant and very separate dogs barking. But to dispel the notion of chance, you may choose the direction from which the dogs are to bark and the size of each dog."

"Can I choose first?" asked the Useless Brother, who was suddenly interested.

"Of course," said Lord Tenbury. "You *are* the Minister of Infernal Affairs, after all."

"I am, aren't I?" he said, pleased with himself, looking out over the battlements and waving a finger in the direction of the kitchens. "I choose a Chihuahua, and from over there."

Perkins concentrated for a moment and pointed two fingers. Almost immediately, there was the sharp bark of a small dog, somewhere quite far away, and from the direction he had indicated.

"That's one," said Boo.

"A Great Dane," said Blix, "from there."

A moment later there were the unmistakable deep, gruff tones of a large dog. The sound was so distant that if there had not been a breeze to bring it to our ears, we may not have heard it at all. Perkins was doing well, and the bark of a cocker spaniel next up was of similar expertise. If it had been any closer, it would not have been distant, and if it had been ten feet farther away, we would not have heard it.

"A bull terrier," I said, for it was my turn to choose the final dog, "from over there."

Perkins was relaxed and on a roll. His magic license was in the bag. Nothing, I thought, could stop us now. He had raised his index fingers to commit his final spell when there was a sharp cough from behind us.

We turned to find a footman dressed in full livery with embroidered jacket, tight red breeches, stockings, and a wig. He held a staff he struck twice on the ground, then announced in a shrill voice, "His Gracious Majesty, King Snodd IV!"

ELEVEN

King Snodd IV

Everyone but the Useless Brother and Boo knelt as the king walked out onto the flat roof. He was on his own. More accurately, he had so few courtiers, hangers-on, and advisors that he might as well have been alone. I counted an astonishingly low dozen, which was normal when the king was in a solitary frame of mind.

Snodd's ridiculously high staffing levels were not unusual for royalty of the Ununited Kingdoms. He reputedly needed four valets to take a bath and a minimum of two to use the lavatory. One to hold the toilet paper and the other to . . . well, I'm sure you get the picture.

It was Tenbury who spoke first.

"Your Highness," he said, "you bless us with your presence."

"I do rather, don't I?" the king replied.

He was a youthful-looking forty and was in annoyingly good health for those who thought it might be better for all concerned if he would drop dead and let his wife, the considerably less militaristic and more diplomatic Queen Mimosa, take over. One of the few acts of civil disobedience in the kingdom in recent years had been a march in support of Queen Mimosa having greater control of government. The king had been prepared to use water cannon, riot police, and tear gas until Queen Mimosa told the marchers to return home and be patient, which they did, much to the king's astonishment and annoyance. He'd not used his riot police for a while and thought they needed some practice.

"I heard my good friend Jennifer Strange was in the castle," said the king, "and I just—Why is that woman not groveling or averting her eyes in my presence?"

We all looked up from where we were kneeling.

"This is the Once Magnificent Boolean Smith, Your Majesty, the magic license adjudicator and recently appointed Beastmaster," Tenbury said.

"What happened to Hugo?"

"He came off worse in an argument with a Tralfamosaur."

The king stared at Boo again and took two steps forward. "Now, listen here, good lady, I am the . . ."

His voice trailed off as he fell into the inky blackness of her eyes.

"Lumme," he said, "I have the queerest feeling that I'm drowning."

"Not yet," replied Once Magnificent Boo in an ominous tone. "But you shall, and in mud, deserted by those you thought were friends."

There was a difficult pause as the king and his courtiers took this in. The fact that there *was* a pause rather than an instant contradiction seemed to suggest that not only the king thought this a feasible demise, but his attendants did, too.

"Now, listen here —" the king repeated.

"Your Majesty should forgive a respected ex-enchantress her eccentricities," said Tenbury in a soothing tone, and whispered something in the king's ear.

"Indeed," said the king. "All may rise, since we are friends together."

We got to our feet. The king cleared his throat and, ignoring Boo, began again.

"I heard my good friend Jennifer was in the castle, and I popped by to say 'Wotcha.'"

I was immediately suspicious. The king never "popped by" anywhere, rarely said "Wotcha," and was *definitely* not a friend.

"Come here, child," said the king, and I approached cautiously. The last time we met he had me put in jail for daring to meddle in his plans to invade the Duchy of Brecon. Thankfully, "averting a war with pacifist thoughts aforethought" couldn't be found anywhere on the statute books, so I was released after two weeks of eating half-rations and sleeping under a single sheet in a damp cell without natural light. To anyone else it might have been unbearable, but after being brought up by the Blessed Ladies of the Lobster, I found it really quite relaxing. I'd not slept so well for months.

"Good afternoon, Your Majesty," I said, curtseying. "How best can I serve you?"

With despots it was always best to flatter and say yes as often as possible. The king smiled, revealing a set of ridiculously white teeth. He wore a monocle and was thought of as handsome for a member of the royalty, and slightly like a weasel for anyone else. He had a silly habit of always wearing a crown, as well as lots of scarlet and ermine.

"I have decided that I should take this Mystical Arts nonsense more seriously than I have in the past," he announced. "And now that the power of your old-fangled magic is arising once more, I must have a dedicated wizard at court in order to see how best the nation's newest asset can be efficiently exploited." He thought for a moment. "I mean, 'how magic can best be used to serve the people.' What do you think?"

"I think that the Mystical Arts are best independent," I replied. "They should serve no one in particular, and be beholden to no —"

"You are but a child," King Snodd said patronizingly. "Simplistic and unversed in the ways of the world. What do you say, All Powerful Blix?"

I thought of mentioning that he was simply the Amazing Blix, but this whole thing seemed to have a degree of stage management about it. There had been negotiations behind my back, and right now I was not guiding events, but a passenger upon them.

"I think that is a fine idea, sire," said Blix obsequiously. "Your Gracious Majesty has a responsibility to better promote this new power for the betterment of the Ununited Kingdoms."

"I could not have put it better myself, and did," said the king, turning back to me. "You are appointed to the post, Mr. Blix. Miss Strange, can I rely upon Kazam to afford all help that Court Mystician All Powerful Blix requires?"

I stared at the king for a moment. Court Mystician was a big jump for Blix — and a worrying one. By ancient decree from the days when wizards were more powerful than they are now, it made him eighth in line to the throne, after the royal family and Lord Tenbury. At times like this, I simply did what the Great Zambini would have done. He had expressly told me that Blix was not to be trusted in any way, shape, or form. I chose my words carefully.

"I'm afraid to say that we would have to rigorously examine any requests from Blix and consider each very carefully on its individual merits."

The king raised an eyebrow. "Is that a yes?"

"No."

The king smiled at me. "You are so very, very predictable, Miss Strange. I could force your house to join, and even enact legislation to have Kazam outlawed. But those are the acts of a despot, not of a fair, just, and much-loved leader. Me," he added, in case I was wondering. "No, I suggest that a new company be formed from Kazam and iMagic, which will be called Snodd Magic PLC. From these fine beginnings great things will be achieved. What do you say?"

I didn't have to choose my words so carefully this time. "I believe I speak for all Kazam's members when I say that I must reluctantly decline Your Majesty's generous offer. We will not support the Amazing Blix in any form whatsoever and will strongly resist any attempt at a merger."

"Is that a no?"

"Yes."

"Oh dear," said the king with a sigh, "an impasse.

What do we do when we reach an impasse, Useless Brother?"

"A what?"

"I'll tell you," continued the king. "We should have a contest to decide the matter. Magical contests are always enjoyed by the unwashed and the destitute—and *especially* by the unwashed destitute. I understand that it is a traditional way to resolve matters between those versed in the Mystical Arts. Is that not so, Court Mystician?"

"Most definitely," said Blix, turning to me. "From the head of one House of Enchantment to another, I challenge Kazam to a contest. Winner takes control of the other's company."

I couldn't really back out. The sorcerer's protocol was obscure, ancient, mostly illogical, and cemented into law by long implementation. To refuse a challenge was unthinkable, but then to *issue* a challenge was also unthinkable—it was the stuff only ill-mannered dopes without any manners would do. Wizards like Blix, in fact.

"I reluctantly accept," I replied, annoyed by the inflexibility of the protocol but not too worried. We could easily outconjure iMagic in any test they chose. "What shall the contest be?"

"Why not Hereford's old bridge?" suggested Tenbury. "Kazam was planning on rebuilding it on Friday, and we can instead have a contest. Kazam can build from the north bank and iMagic from the south. First one to get its keystones fitted in the center of the middle arch wins the contest. Magic License Adjudicator, is that fair?"

"As fair as you'll see in this kingdom," said the Once Magnificent Boo, which I *think* meant she agreed.

"I agree to the terms," said Blix with a smile I didn't much care for. "Jennifer?"

"I, too, agree," I said, "on the proviso that if Kazam wins, the position of Court Mystician is taken up by someone of our choosing."

"Very well," said the king. "Blix, you agree to this?"

"I agree."

"What's a keystone?" asked the King's Useless Brother.

"Well, there it is, then," said King Snodd, ignoring him entirely. "Carry on." And he swept from the roof with his entourage.

A contest was always stressful, but we weren't in much trouble. Even with Lady Mawgon as alabaster we still had five sorcerers to their three, if Perkins could finish the test. Besides, dealing with Blix and the rabble over at iMagic once and for all might actually help matters.

"Well," said Blix, "may the best side win."

"We plan to," I replied.

"Can we finish the application?" asked the Useless Brother. "I'm keen to use that stamp."

"A bull terrier," I said after a brief pause, "from Dorstonville."

Unfazed, Perkins gesticulated with his fingers, and far away a bull terrier barked.

"The test is complete to my satisfaction," announced Boo. She signed the form awkwardly with her gloved hands and left without a further word to any of us.

The form was duly countersigned by the King's Useless Brother, and the heavy rubber stamp descended. We stayed for a few minutes in the outer office while the paperwork was processed, and twenty minutes later we were back outside, where Tiger was waiting for us in the Volkswagen.

"How did it go?" he asked.

Perkins showed him the certificate, and Tiger congratulated him. We all talked about the contest on the journey back to Zambini Towers.

"I've never seen a wizidrical contest before," said Tiger.

"Few have," I replied, "and although they're an unwelcome distraction, they never fail to be anything but dramatic."

"The most spectacular contest was chronicled in the seventeenth century by Dude the Obscure," said Perkins, who was more up on this sort of stuff, "and was between the Mighty Shandar and the Truly Awesome Spontini. Shandar won three forests to a seven-headed dog in the first round but lost nine castles to a geyser of lemonade in the second. It has been calculated that the deciding round used more than half a gigashandar an hour and involved some deft transformations, several vanishings, an exciting and wholly unrepeatable global teleport chase, and an ice storm in summer. It was said the crackle was depleted so completely that no useful magic was done anywhere in the world for more than six months."

"Who won?" asked Tiger.

"The Mighty Shandar," replied Perkins. "Who else?"

"Spectacular, perhaps," I said, "but the most nail-biting was reputedly a low-level contest between two Spellmanagers of middle ranking who simply had an armchair hover-off in 1911. First one to touch the ground in his or her armchair lost. It was won after seventy-six hours of eye-popping concentration by Lady Chumpkin of Spode, who apparently lost nearly fifty pounds with the effort."

"Will we win the bridge contest?" asked Tiger.

"Without a doubt," I said, with not quite as much certainty as I wished.

TWELVE

Shifting Oaks

We'd had lunch, congratulated Perkins, and were now gathered in the Palm Court. The only member of the inner sanctum of licensed sorcerers absent was Patrick of Ludlow, who was busy moving an oak for a wealthy client eager to alphabetize his arboretum.

Lady Mawgon and Monty Vanguard were still there, exactly the same as when we left. It would take ten or twenty years before a thin coating of lichen would make them look any different, although they might need a dusting by next Tuesday.

"Goodness," said Perkins, who'd never seen a spell go so wrong before. "Have we attempted a Magnaflux Reversal?"

"Several times."

"Has anyone asked the Mysterious X?" suggested Half Price. "Since it's less of a who and more a what, it might have a different take on the problem."

This was entirely true. Because of Mysterious X's nebulous state of semi-existence, we often gave it small jobs such as rescuing cats stuck up trees; it could persuade pianos into tune by glaring at them. The fact that it didn't have a license didn't bother us, as there was little tangible evidence to say X even existed at all.

"I could speak to it," volunteered Tiger. "I think it quite likes me."

"Go on, then," said Wizard Moobin. As Tiger hurried off, he passed the Transient Moose, who had just reappeared in the doorway and was watching us all in his usual laconic manner.

"Let's talk about the bridge contest," I announced. "Let's suppose we can't get Lady Mawgon back or use the Dibbles to help us. What problems do you think we might have?"

"We're still five to their three," said Moobin. "Blix is about on a par with me and a powerful levitator, but both Tchango and Dame Corby are less powerful than the Price brothers. Patrick is a solid plodder and can be trusted to get any heavy stone into position. We can keep Perkins in reserve and still beat them comfortably."

They then went on about crackle allocations, and

although half my attention was on the meeting, my mind tends to wander during technical discussions. As I looked around the room, my gaze fell upon the Transient Moose, who sniffed delicately at the area where the rent had been. I narrowed my eyes. For as long as anyone could remember, the moose had simply stood around doing not very much at all. As I watched, he faded from view, not to another part of the hotel as he usually did but to where Lady Mawgon was rooted to the spot in her calcite splendor. The moose stared at the alabaster, shook his antlers, and then vanished.

"Did you see that?"

"See what?" asked Moobin, who had just launched into a long and tedious discussion about Zorff's Sixth Axiom.

"The moose. He was examining Lady Mawgon as though he were . . . aware."

"Moose was written with Mandrake Sentience Emulation Protocols," said Full Price, "and like a Quarkbeast shows considerable evidence of consciousness. But as to whether he is *really* alive or designed to make us think he is, we'll never really know."

I opened my mouth to answer but then noticed Tiger waving at me from the door of the Palm Court. I excused myself and hurried over, glad for a distraction.

"Problems?"

"Could be," he said. "Patrick of Ludlow just phoned. He said he's run into oversurge issues moving the oak in the arboretum over in Holme Lacy. He wants a wizard to go down and help sort things out."

"If it's an oversurge issue, why not take Perkins?" said Moobin when I asked him if he could help. "He should learn what it's like to absorb crackle rather than use it."

Perkins agreed wholeheartedly, as he was eager to begin his new career as a sorcerer. A few minutes later Perkins, Tiger, and I were walking out the door toward my car. Tiger was carrying a partially inflated trash bag, as this was how the Mysterious X traveled outside Zambini Towers. When you were nothing more than an inexplicable energy field of unknown origin, even a light breeze has an unsettling dispersing effect.

"Can you drop us off at the zoo?" asked Tiger. "I kind of get the idea that Mysterious X *might* be able to help with the whole RUNIX deal but wants to see the new buzonji cub first."

That was how the Mysterious X communicated: not by words but by ideas that popped into your head. Perkins had spent many hours consulting with him on the powers of suggestion—or, if you didn't believe in Mysterious X, Perkins had been sitting in a room mumbling to himself.

"I never thought X was big on zoos," I said as we climbed into my car, "but then again, the buzonji cub is *very* cute. All gangly legs and a pink nose."

I dropped Tiger and the Mysterious X at Hereford Zoo. While disappointingly without an elephant or any penguins, the zoo was saved from ignominy because it had several animals created by magic. Back in the days of almost unbridled power, Super Grand Master Sorcerers would attempt to outdo one another in their creation of weird and wonderful beasts. Of the seventeen known non-evolutionary creatures, only eight still existed. Hereford Zoo had an unprecedented four, including the only captive breeding pair of buzonji, sort of a six-legged okapi, and two species of shridloo, a desert and dessert — the latter being the edible variety. The only captive Tralfamosaur was here, and had been placed in a more secure compound after it ate the previous Beastcatcher. A frazzle named Devlin completed the small collection; it was not just the only specimen living outside its natural habitat of the wetlands of Norfolk, but also the only one glad about it. There used to be a Quarkbeast, but it kept frightening people, so was removed from display.

"So how should I handle an oversurge?" asked Perkins as we drove out of Hereford toward Colonel Bloch-Draine's country estate at Holme Lacy.

"Surges are unpredictable and pretty useless, like the

wasted heat in a steam engine, so what you have to do is redirect the crackle elsewhere, like a safety valve. It can be quite fun, apparently—spelling anything just to use up the power. Showers of toads, levitation, whatever strikes your fancy."

"A sort of magic free lunch?"

"Kind of, except you still have to fill out the form B1-7G. If the paperwork isn't in order, the penalties are severe. The rules against illegal sorcery are quite fourteenth-century."

"Don't worry. I won't let you or Kazam down."

There was quiet for a moment as we drove down the road.

"Jenny?"

"Yes?"

"Have you considered my offer to go and see the Jimmy Nuttjob stunt show?"

I looked across at him. "Is this a date?"

"Might be," he said, staring at his feet.

I said the first thing that came into my head. "I just turned sixteen. I'm too young."

"Let's be honest, you don't act much like a sixteen-year-old, what with the responsibility and dealing with Blix and matters of ethics and whatnot."

"It's a foundling thing," I told him. "You grow up quick when you have to fight every night with forty other girls for the only handkerchief in the orphanage."

"To blow your nose?"

"To use as a pillow. You're just going to have to be careful with . . . relationships when you're a sorcerer. People can sometimes get sniffy and wonder what they saw in you, and this can lead to accusations of beguiling. It's not provable, but it's bad publicity, and there's always the faint possibility of being hunted down by a crowd of angry and ignorant villagers, all holding torches aloft and imprisoning you in an old windmill that they set on fire."

"Worst-case scenario?"

"Yes."

"Do you think I'm beguiling you?"

I looked across at him and smiled. "If you are, you're not that good at it."

"Ah," Perkins said, and lapsed into silence.

Holme Lacy was less than ten miles away, and we pulled into the imposing front entrance of the colonel's residence a quarter of an hour later. Perkins looked nervously out the window. It was his first gig. Up until now it had just been observation, practice spells at Zambini Towers, and a lot of classroom theory. And surges could be tricky.

I parked the car outside the imposing eighteen-room mansionette. Lieutenant Colonel Sir Reginald George Stamford Bloch-Draine had been one of King Snodd's most faithful military leaders and had personally led a squadron of landships during the Fourth Troll War twelve years before.

The point of the Fourth Troll War had been pretty much the same as the first three: to push the trolls back into the far north and teach them a lesson "once and for all." To this end, the nations of the Ununited Kingdoms had put aside their differences, sending 147 landships on a frontal assault to "soften up" the trolls before the infantry invaded the following week. The landships had breached the first Troll Wall at Stirling and arrived at the second Troll Wall eighteen hours later. They reportedly opened the Troll Gates, and then — nothing. All the radios went dead. Faced with uncertainty and the possible loss of the landships, the generals decided to instigate the ever popular Let's Panic plan and ordered the infantry to attack.

Of the quarter million men and women in action during the twenty-six-minute war that followed, only nine were not lost or eaten. Colonel Bloch-Draine was one of them, saved by an unavoidable dentist appointment that had him away from his landship at the crucial moment of advance. He retired soon after to devote his time to killing and mounting rare creatures before they went extinct. He had recently started collecting trees and saw no reason why this activity shouldn't be exactly the same as collecting stuffed animals: lots of swapping and putting them in alphabetical groups. Clearly, moving trees around his estate was not something he could do on his own, and that was the reason Kazam had been employed.

Patrick of Ludlow was waiting for us outside the colonel's mansionette.

"Apologies for calling you out, Miss Strange," he said, wringing his hands nervously as we got out of the car. "But things aren't doing as they should."

"No problem," I said soothingly. "You and I and Perkins will sort it out."

Patrick could levitate up to seven tons when humidity was low and he was feeling good, which was more often now that his six-ounce-a-day marzipan habit was well behind him. He was a simple soul, kindly and gentle despite his large size and misshapen appearance. Like most Movers, he had muscles where he shouldn't — grouped around his ankles, wrists, toes, fingers, and the back of his head. His hand looked like a boiled ham with fingertips stuck on randomly. He generally stayed hidden when he wasn't working, in case he might be mistaken for an infant troll.

"What's the problem, Pat?" I asked.

"Problem?" came a voice behind us. "Problem? I expect no problems, only solutions!"

We turned to find the colonel, who despite his retirement still wore a military uniform. On his chest was an impressive array of brightly colored ribbons, each representing a military campaign he had somehow missed due to some unforeseen prior engagement.

"Gadzooks!" he said when he saw me. "A girlie. Bit young for this sort of work, eh?"

I ignored him and stared at his florid features. He had a large mustache, and his eyes were wide and very blue. Oddly, they seemed to have no real life to them—looking into them was like staring at a creepily lifelike waxwork.

"Mr. Perkins and I are here to ensure the oak moving goes as planned. It goes without saying that this is all within the price we quoted."

"Oh," he said, "right. Do you take tea?"

I thanked him and said that we did, to which he replied that he was only asking me. After I'd persuaded him that tea for all of us would get the job completed that much more quickly, he trotted off indoors.

"So," I said, turning back to Patrick, "what's the problem?"

Patrick beckoned me across to the colonel's arboretum, a small spinney of trees surrounding a lake. He indicated two large holes in the ground fifty yards apart. One was presumably where the oak had been and the other where it was meant to end up.

"Everything was going as planned," said Patrick.

"But just as I'd gotten the oak halfway from one place to the other, I had a surge and—well, can you see over there?"

He pointed to the far shore of the lake. Lying lakeside was the oak tree, roots and all.

"That's about half a mile away," said Perkins.

"I surged," said Patrick simply, "and then every time I tried to move the oak closer, the power just leaped and I dumped it even farther away."

"Okay," I said, "this is what we'll do. Patrick, I want you to walk around the lake, lift the oak, and bring it back. If you get another oversurge, I want Perkins to channel the excess into anything he wants. Questions?"

"What should I channel the oversurge into?"

"See how many fish you can lift out of the lake."

Perkins looked at the lake, then at his fingers. Levitation was something he could do.

I stood and watched them walk off around the lake, then heard a noise on the wind—something odd and familiar that I couldn't quite place. I walked across the lawn toward a rusty battle tank that the colonel had transformed into a tasteless garden feature with the addition of several potted plants and a Virginia creeper on the gun barrel.

"Who's there?" I asked, and heard a rustling.

I pushed aside the azaleas and walked behind the armored vehicle, where I found a pile of grass clippings and a compost heap. Nothing looked even remotely unusual, but as I was leaving I noticed that one of the tank's heavy tracks had been chewed, and recently. I peered more closely at the tooth marks, then searched the soft earth near my feet.

I soon found what I was looking for: several dull metal ball bearings of varying size. I picked them up and moved farther into the scrubby woodland, but after searching for five minutes and finding nothing more, I returned to wait for Patrick and Perkins to bring the oak back, which they did without any problems at all. The oak fitted snugly in its new hole, and the earth was soon moved in.

"Easy as winking," said Patrick, "without any surging at all. I guess you guys had a wasted journey."

"Never a waste, Patrick," I said thoughtfully. "Call us anytime."

"Sorry for the delay," said the colonel as he returned with the tea things. "I made some scones. Good job with the oak. Have you time to move the silver birch twelve feet to its left?"

"You'll have to rebook, sir; we have quite a full—"

"Where did you get those?" The colonel was staring at the ball bearings I had found behind the tank. I knew what they were, but I hadn't expected him to. They were cadmium-coated cupro-nickel spheres with a zinc core.

"Quarkbeast droppings!" exclaimed the colonel.

"I've been after a Quark for years. I must fetch my dart gun." And he was off, running surprisingly fast for a seventy-year-old.

With a Quarkbeast on the loose and a colonel with an itchy trigger finger, this was something I wanted to do on my own. I suggested to Perkins and Patrick — told them, actually — that they return to Kazam and lend their minds to the depetrification of Lady Mawgon.

"Where's the odd-looking fella and the young one with the sticky-out ears?" asked the colonel when he had returned with his gun.

"The next job," I replied, but the colonel wasn't listening. With his hunting instincts all aquiver, he had already loaded the weapon with two large tranquilizer darts.

"Tipped with carbide steel," explained the colonel, "to penetrate their hide."

"While I applaud your efforts to *not* kill it," I said, "may I ask what you are thinking of doing with an unconscious Quarkbeast?"

"Do you know how much people will pay to hunt for Quarks?" he said with a grin. "The king's deer park over at Moccas would be an admirable base from which to run hunting trips."

"They'll be hard to catch," I said.

"I'm counting on it. I might get ten or more hunts out of it before the blighter is finally bagged. Now, listen, girlie," he continued. "I need to know all about Quark-beasts. What they like, what they dislike. Best way to sneak up on one, favorite color, that kind of stuff."

"Why don't you speak to the Once Magnificent Boo?" I replied. "She runs a Quarkbeast rescue center west of town."

"I tried, but Miss Smith is somewhat . . . angry," admitted the colonel. "I thought I might get more sense out of you. And don't pretend you know nothing about them. Your affection for the little beasts is well documented. There's a bronze statue outside Zambini Towers, for goodness' sake, put there by you and your wizardy chums."

I could have told him many things. About how they like to chew on scrap metal and aren't particularly fussy — except about lead, which gets stuck between their teeth, and cobalt, which gives them the runs. I could have told him how they change color when they get emotional or how they need fish oil to keep their scales shiny or how they like a walk twice daily. I might have told him that they are loyal, rarely eat cats, and, despite appearances, are warm and faithful companions that it would be an honor to walk alongside. I could have said all that, but I didn't.

I said this: "They can chew their way through a dou-ble-decker bus lengthwise in less than eight seconds, and know when they are being tracked. If threatened, they will launch a preemptive attack with a degree of savagery that would make a Berzerker faint. You don't want to be hunting Quarkbeast, Colonel."

"Yes, yes, whatever you say. Now, be quiet. I don't want to lose it."

And so saying, he began to track the Quarkbeast, and I followed him. If there was a chance to put off his aim or alert the beast, I would take it. The tracking was quite easy, as beasts can rarely pass any metal without a quick bite to see whether it would make a good snack. We passed a sheet of nibbled corrugated iron, a bitten wire fence, and an abandoned car with the chrome licked off the bumpers.

The colonel dropped to one knee and peered around carefully. "What's that noise?"

"I didn't hear anything."

Actually, I had. When the colonel turned the other way, I leaned across and peered in the open window of the abandoned car. The intelligent mauve eyes of a Quarkbeast stared back at me. The leathery scales that covered its back were partially raised in defense, and acidic drops of saliva hissed upon the corroded metal. I placed my finger to my lips, and it wagged its tail twice to say that it understood. This was bad news, as Quarkbeasts have weighted tails, and it thumped against the old car like a drum.

In an instant the colonel had spotted the Quarkbeast and raised the gun to his shoulder. But before he could fire, there was a bright flash of green and a deep *whoompa* noise—and in an instant, the colonel and I were rolling end over end in the long grass.

I sat up and looked around. The Quarkbeast had vanished, but that wasn't all that had changed. The abandoned car—every last mangled part of it—was now perfectly transformed into caramelized sugar, and the grass in the immediate vicinity was bright blue. I looked at the colonel, who now had his undershirt and boxer shorts on the *outside* of his uniform. I was grateful that this had not happened to me, but I had not been totally spared: My clothes were now on backwards, which was uncomfortable and disconcerting.

"What was that?" asked the colonel, who seemed unconcerned that I now knew he had dancing hippos on his underwear.

"I have no idea at all," I told him as I picked myself up. "Nope, none. None at all. Nothing whatever. Zip."

"Hmm," said the colonel. "Think the Quarkbeast is gone?"

"Long gone."

I walked with him back to the house and borrowed the downstairs bathroom to put my clothes back on the right way—and was mildly perturbed to realize that my clothes had been untouched and *I* had been mirrored. I was now right-handed, and the small mole on my left cheek was now on my right. I'd have to ask Moobin if there might be any long-term health issues.

I drove back to Zambini Towers deep in thought, mostly about the Quarkbeast. I had lied when I told the colonel I didn't know what we'd just witnessed. The beast had escaped in a short burst of wizidrical energy that had caused randomized passive spelling, resulting in the caramelized steel, clothing manipulation, and my mirroring. Why it might suddenly do this, I had no idea.

Quarkbeasts were weird, but up until now, I'd had no idea *how* weird.

THIRTEEN

The King's Address

I wandered into the Palm Court as soon as I got home to see if anyone had managed to unravel Lady Mawgon or unlock the passthought. No one had. Full Price was there among a pile of old books attempting to figure out a solution, and just to add more frustration to the mix, the Dibble Storage Coils were now at sixty percent capacity and still rising. When they were full they would vent crackle and start to make cloud shapes over Zambini Towers. But with no way to use the power, it would be magic wasted, and even if we *could* get the Dibbles online, they'd be useless without Lady Mawgon.

"Any idea what caused the surge?" Full Price asked.

"No," I replied. "It had gone by the time we got there."

"You look different."

"I got mirrored by a sudden burst of wizidrical power."

"From what?"

"A Quarkbeast escaping in a panic. Did you know they could cause that?"

"No—but then there's much we don't know about them," said Full, returning to his work.

"Is it dangerous?" I asked.

"Is what dangerous?" he asked, without looking up.

"Being reversed."

"Not at all. We could try and change you back, but as with all complex procedures, there are risks. Unless you're unhappy, I'd stay as you are."

I told Full Price I'd see how it felt being right-handed and let him know, then went to the Kazam offices, where I found Kevin Zipp staring into space.

"Anything?" I asked.

"I'm afraid not," replied Kevin. "A possible winner at the three twenty at Haydock Park, something about a friend hidden behind a green door, and that warning about Vision Boss again."

"But nothing about the Great Zambini?"

He shook his head, so I jotted what he'd seen in the Visions Book under codes RAD097 to RAD099.

I was doing paperwork and dealing with messages when Tiger reappeared, inflated trash bag in hand.

"How did the Mysterious X like the zoo?" I asked.

"So-so," he replied, "but then it seemed to be saying that going to a movie might also help clear its mind, so I took it to see *Rupert the Foundling Conquers the Universe*."

"Hmm," I mused, wondering if Mysterious X was simply milking the situation to get a day out. Unsurprisingly, the Mysterious X often worked in mysterious ways. "Is X any closer to helping us?"

"I don't think so."

"It was worth a try. You better put it back in its room."

"Okay," said Tiger, and walked off.

Perkins and Patrick wandered in and presented their B1-7G forms to be processed. The bureaucracy was as boring as dusting but, like dusting, necessary.

"Your first form," I said to Perkins, stamping and countersigning B1-7G. "Congratulations. You can get your mother to stick it on the fridge."

Supper was always early, and once the jam roly-poly had been left uneaten for the sixty-eighth consecutive day (a new record), Moobin had all those involved in the bridge gig convene in the Palm Court. Both Full and Half were there, as well as Patrick, Perkins, me, and Tiger—and Lady Mawgon and Monty Vanguard, but strictly in a non-speaking capacity. We were there partly to have a meeting and partly to watch a repeat of the king's early evening Television Address to the People.

He usually used the address to tell citizens to consume less water or buy more shares in Snodd Industries, or simply to announce another tedious milestone in Princess Shazza's very public upbringing. Today's big news, however, was that Conrad Blix had been named Court Mystician. Blix was there on the screen next to the king, trying to appear dignified and stately but actually looking smug and odious.

"It was to be expected," I said sadly. "The king likes to publicize almost everything he does."

"I know," said Moobin, "but look carefully in the background."

We leaned closer as he ran the six-minute address again. As usual, the address was filmed wherever the king happened to be, surrounded by whomever he happened to be with. On this occasion he was naming a new landship, and there, standing suspiciously close, was the King's Useless Brother, Lord Tenbury — and Mr. Trimble.

"Looks like BellShout Communications is covering all bases," I murmured.

Mr. Trimble had been sounding me out earlier for Kazam's feelings about reactivating the mobile phone network, and I had foolishly given him a straight answer: that attempting to administer such a fundamental force would be like trying to tax gravity or own the stars. What we saw on TV confirmed what we all suspected — the king was attempting to control the administration of magic for financial ends, and with the help of Blix and Lord Tenbury. They could name their own price to Mr. Trimble and BellShout Communications. And that would just be the beginning. Magic for sale to the highest bidder.

"We *really* need to win the contest on Friday, don't we?" said Perkins.

"Definitely," said Moobin as he switched off the TV. "There's a lot riding on it. It's not just about the ownership of Kazam; it's about the ownership of magic itself."

We fell silent, thinking about what the magic industry would be like run by the king and Blix. It wasn't a happy scenario, no matter how upbeat you tried to be. Quite the opposite — it would be a disaster.

"We'll win easily as long as we keep our heads," said Moobin breezily, pointing at two pictures of the bridge. One was as it should look, all nice and neat, and another how it looked now — several hundred tons of damp slippery rubble. "It'll be a standard lift and fix, with two teams working in pairs. One to raise the stones from the riverbed, and the other to hold them in position while the first speed-sets the mortar. I suggest Perkins and Full on one team and Half and Patrick on the other. I'll be on hand to offer assistance wherever it is needed and to direct the operation. We shouldn't have any problems, but we should all practice tomorrow and keep trying to get Mawgon back, who despite being a monumental pain in the backside is actually a first-class sorcerer. Jennifer has some ideas on this. Jenny?"

I stood up and cleared my throat. "Kevin Zipp has prophesied that the Great Zambini will return tomorrow at four-oh-three p.m. for a few minutes. I've got the prince shadowing Zipp, and as soon as we have a location for Mr. Zambini's reappearance, I'll get straight over there. My primary goal will be to learn how to unlock Lady Mawgon and the Dibble Storage Coils, and after that, to try and help Zambini not disappear again."

"Good," said Moobin. "Any questions?"

"Yes," said Tiger. "Why do *inflammable* and *flammable* mean the same thing?"

"Sorry, I should rephrase that: Any questions relating to the job at hand?"

There weren't.

"Well," said Moobin with finality, "there it is, then. Rest well."

FOURTEEN

The Perfidy Begins

Sleep was fitful and restless, and from the wee hours I was reduced to staring at the fireflies that flickered at the window, feeding off the gentle buzz of wizidrical energy that leaked out of the building.

Once a reasonable hour had arrived, I took a bath and went downstairs. I found the Youthful Perkins and Patrick of Ludlow in the lobby, busily building a practice arch out of some cobbles. It was a tricky act, and one that required not only good coordination but teamwork. They had to hold all the cobbles in a semicircle until the final one — the keystone — was placed at the apex, at which point they could both relax and the arch would stay up on its own.

Trouble was, it didn't seem to want to. On the few occasions they managed to get a complete arch made, it tumbled down as soon as they relaxed.

"It will be easier with bigger stones and the abutments to take the outward forces," said Perkins, and Patrick grunted in agreement.

I had some breakfast and went to the office to check on Kevin Zipp. He was still asleep. Owen of Rhayder was standing by on Kevin watch for a few hours, while Prince Nasil ran some errands. Owen was our second carpeteer and, through no fault of his own, the lesser of the two. While the prince's carpet was a frayed and moth-bitten artifact that would make the inside of a dumpster look tidy, Owen's was eight times worse. A carpet's design life was twenty thousand hours or three centuries before remanufacture, and Owen's was well beyond both.

"Did Kevin say anything in his sleep?" I asked.

"Not much," replied Owen. "Just mumblings about index fingers, the Tralfamosaur, important people being blown to bits, and how ice cream will be on the menu more than once a month this time next year."

"I like the sound of that," said Tiger, who had just wandered in.

"I hope you're referring to the ice cream and not the blowing to bits. Put the visions in the book, will you? I think we're at RAD099. I'm going to have a look at the contest preparations."

I stepped out of the hotel onto Snodd Lane and walked to where it widened out into Snodd Street before turning left onto Snodd Boulevard. I picked up a copy of the *Hereford Daily Eyestrain* from the seller on the corner and noted without much surprise that the competition was headline news.

TWO HOUSES BATTLE FOR TOP WIZ SLOT

The article was more or less correct but heavily skewed in favor of Blix, whom the state-controlled paper described as "newly appointed Court Mystician"; it also repeated the incorrect All Powerful accolade. Further down they referred to him as "a *very* distant relative of Blix the Hideously Barbarous" and then quoted him as saying that "the forces of good must be properly managed for the benefit of the people." I went and gave the newspaper back to the seller and skillfully negotiated a partial refund, then made my way to the wrecked bridge.

There had been many attempts to shame King Snodd into footing the bill for repairs after the bridge's collapse. The most persuasive argument was that without the bridge there was nowhere to dangle the corpses of the recently executed, as local city health ordinances forbade it within the city limits. To be honest, no one had been executed for almost two decades, as it was considered unfashionable these days; perhaps this was the reason the king hadn't ordered a rebuild.

I stood at the abutment on the north end and looked at the large heap of rubble that stretched all the way to the opposite bank. There had been four piers, and although they still projected about a yard above the water line, most of the stone was now in the riverbed. Working in water was always difficult, as it was a poor conductor of wizidrical energy. Moving a block of masonry one yard in water would take as much energy as moving a block fifty yards on dry land.

SnoddScaffolding, Inc., had already constructed a footbridge across the river to enable the sorcerers to better survey the rubble and was now hastily erecting the tiered seating and royal box. I went and found the Minister for Glee, who was discussing with his staff how best to accommodate the most people, how much they could charge them for seats, popcorn, and hot dogs, and what concessions to give to the unwashed and destitute—if any.

After introductions I explained that due to health and safety considerations all observers would have to be at least fifty yards away to guard against secondary enchantments that split off the main weave.

"Fifty yards?" repeated the minister. "That's not really a close-up view of anything. The king himself insisted on a ringside seat to watch the action at close range."

"It's your call," I said, "but I'm not going to be the one who has to explain why His Gracious Majesty and the royal family will be spending the next two weeks with donkeys' heads."

There was a pause.

"Donkeys' heads?"

"Or two noses. Perhaps worse."

"Fifty yards, you say?"

"Fifty yards."

There was little to be gained from hanging around there, so I walked back to Kazam, stopping on the way to buy some licorice for no reason other than I liked licorice. The candy store was next to Vision Boss, and thinking of Kevin's prediction, I went into the shop and looked around. Vision Boss was a popular chain of opticians, with a huge array of frames to choose from. Everything seemed normal enough, and after digging out my shandarmeter to test for any wizidrical hot spots and finding none, I wandered out again. That was the problem with pre-cogs. You rarely knew the meaning of their visions until it was too late. Sometimes it was better not to know at all.

"Ah!" said a familiar voice as soon as I stepped outside. "Good to see you again, girlie." It was Colonel

Bloch-Draine. He was dressed for hunting this time and carrying his dart gun.

"You're very patronizing," I pointed out.

"Very clever of you to notice, girlie. Have a look at this."

He produced an official-looking certificate that told me he had been engaged by Court Mystician Blix as a "licensed agent" to personally oversee the capture of any "rogue or feral magicozoological beasts terrorizing the city or causing public unease."

"So you and Blix aim to start Quarkbeast-hunting tours?" I asked, putting two and two together.

"The tourism sector is an underexploited resource in this kingdom," the colonel said. "The Cambrian Empire earns more than eight million moolah in Tralfamosaur hunts alone."

"Which eat those same hunters on a regular basis, I've heard."

"We will insist on payment in advance," replied the colonel, who was clearly of a practical, if callous, frame of mind. "Now, where would I find a Quarkbeast?"

"I can't help you, Colonel."

"You *can* help me," he replied, "and will. Failure to assist a royal agent in the execution of lawful duties is an offense punishable by two years in prison with hard labor."

I stared at him for a moment and decided to call his bluff. "Then you will have to have me arrested, Colonel."

He looked at me, and a faint smile crossed his lined features.

"You have spirit," he said at last, "and I respect that. Are you lined up for a husband yet? My third son is still without a wife."

It wasn't an unusual question; in the Kingdom of Snodd ninety-five percent of marriages were arranged. The only benefit of being an orphan was that you were entitled to arrange your own.

"Three possibles with five in reserve," I said, lying through my teeth.

"Can I put my son down as sixth reserve?" he asked.

"No."

"He has six acres and a steady job in waste disposal — *and* all his own teeth."

"How tempting," I replied, "but still no."

"Tarquin will be disappointed."

"I daresay I can live with that."

The colonel thought for a moment. "Are you sure you won't help me find the Quarkbeast?"

"I would rather sunbathe in the Tralfamosaur enclosure draped in bacon."

"I don't need your help anyway," he said at last. "I

have what information I need from the All Powerful Blix. Good day, Miss Strange. You'll regret not considering Tarquin."

And he hurried off in the direction of the bridge.

"It's the *Amazing* Blix!" I called out after him, but to no avail. I shrugged and turned for home.

As soon as I stepped into Zambini Towers, I knew something was wrong. Wizard Moobin was sitting in a chair in the lobby, looking worried.

"Problems?" I asked.

"Full and Half Price have been arrested pending extradition to face charges in the Cambrian Empire," replied Moobin sadly. "It is alleged they were key figures in Cambria's illegal Thermowizidrical Explosive Device program in the eighties, as banned by the Genevieve Convention of 1922."

"Is that serious?"

"It's a crime against Harmony — the worst sort. It carries a double death with added death penalty."

"That's insane!" I replied. "The Prices wouldn't hurt a fly. This is all totally trumped up, right?"

Moobin didn't say anything. He just sat there and bit his lip.

"Blast," I said under my breath, knowing from his look that this was *precisely* what the Prices had been fleeing when they arrived at Kazam twenty years before. The

Great Zambini had given shelter to all those versed in the Mystical Arts, regardless of their past. I shuddered as I thought about who else we might have in the building, and what they might have done.

"We can still win the contest," said Moobin. "Me, Patrick, and Perkins against Blix, Corby, and Tchango. Look at it this way: Three against three is a fair fight."

"With the greatest respect," I replied, "Blix is not after a fair fight. He won't stop until it's his three against our one — or less."

We sat in silence in the empty lobby, the only sounds the clock, the rustling of oak leaves, and the occasional *pop* as the Transient Moose moved in and out. Things didn't look great, to be honest — and I knew who was to blame.

"I'm sorry," I said at last.

"What for?"

"For agreeing to this contest."

"You didn't have any option," said Moobin, placing his hand on my arm. "A challenge is a challenge. The real fault lies with Blix. How long do you think it will be before they arrest the next one of us?"

"Any minute now, I should imagine."

Just as I spoke, Detective Villiers and Sergeant Norton walked in the front door. If there was work of a dubious nature that needed a veneer of legality to be done, these two would be doing it.

"Miss Strange," said Detective Villiers. "How delightful to meet you again."

I didn't have time for this. "Where are the Prices?" I demanded.

Villiers and Norton gave me their well-practiced triumphant grin.

"Under lock and key until the hearing on Monday," said Sergeant Norton, who was the physical opposite of Villiers—heavy in body and face to Norton's almost painful thinness. We often joked that they were the before and after in a weight-loss ad. I'd crossed swords with them in the past, and didn't like them.

"Monday? Conveniently three days *after* the bridge gig?"

"These are serious charges, Miss Strange. But we're not here for idle chitchat."

"No?" I thought they had come for me because I'd refused to help hunt Quarkbeast, but they hadn't. Maybe the colonel wanted to keep me sweet for the Tarquin option.

"Wizard Gareth Archibald Moobin?" asked Villiers in that way police do when they already know the answer.

"You know I am."

"You're under arrest for committing an illegal act of magic; for failing to declare said act of magic; for not submitting the relevant paperwork; for plotting to hide said act of magic from the authorities."

Norton took Moobin's arm. I figured they knew he could teleport and weren't going to risk losing him.

"And what act was this?" I asked, knowing full well that in the four years I had been at Kazam not a single act of sorcery had gone unrecorded.

"It's about a bunch of roses produced 'from thin air' as a gift to a certain Miss Bancroft," said Norton, "on or around October twenty-third, 1988."

"Jessica," said Moobin in a quiet voice.

"Yes," said Norton. "Jessica."

Moobin looked at me and shrugged while they slipped lead-lined cuffs onto his index fingers to keep him from spelling.

"Bet you regret trying to impress her now, eh?" sneered Villiers.

"Oddly, no," Moobin admitted with a fond smile. "She was quite something. What we call a refuzic—possessed of magical powers but convinced she had none. Get this: She could lick a man's bald head and tell what he had for breakfast. Don't tell me that's not magic. What's she doing these days?"

"She's Mrs. Villiers," said Villiers, "and if you go spreading the bald-head thing around, it won't be just the king and Blix playing 'jail the wizard.'"

"Hey, Officer," said Tiger, who had just walked in, "I can make a bacon roll vanish—and then make it reappear the following morning in a completely different form. You going to arrest me for illegal wizardry, too?"

Norton and Villiers glared at Tiger, appalled at his gross impertinence. If they'd not been busy, they would have arrested him, too.

"Bloody foundlings," said Norton. "A waste of space, all of you. One more thing: If you're looking for Patrick of Ludlow, don't. We just picked him up, too — on charges relating to marzipan abuse. So long, Jenny."

And a moment later the doors were swinging shut behind them.

"This is all my fault," I said, sitting down and putting my face in my hands. It was now Perkins up against the powers of Blix and his cronies. One of ours against three of theirs.

"It's not your fault and it could be worse," said Tiger in a soothing voice.

"How could it possibly be worse?"

"It could be Friday. It isn't. It's only Thursday morning. Lots can happen. So we're down to only one sorcerer. Big deal. There must be others we can use."

"No one else has a license."

"What about sorcerers who had licenses from the old days? Ones who never had them taken away?"

"If they were sane enough to work, they would be."

Tiger nodded toward the front door. "I wasn't thinking of in here. I was thinking of . . . out there."

I sat up. Hope had not yet fully departed.

"You're right. There are two I could try. I'll start with Mother Zenobia."

"Would she help us?"

"Almost certainly not—but it's worth a shot. And listen, if Blix wants to play dirty, so should we."

"Meaning?"

"Meaning we should find out something about him. Something we can use against him. Past misdemeanors, dirt, unpaid parking tickets—I don't know. You do some snooping, and I'll try and rustle up some sorcerers."

I walked out the front entrance, realized I'd forgotten my keys, turned around, pushed open the door to Zambini Towers—and found myself stepping out the back of the hotel. I held the door wide open, and, impossibly, the front entrance led straight out the back. It was as if Zambini Towers wasn't there at all. I closed the door again and pressed the doorbell.

The door was answered by Perkins, and oddly, he was inside—behind him I could see the lobby.

"Forget your keys?"

"Look at this."

He stepped out and I closed the door, then told him to open it. He did so, and stared not at the lobby but at the alleyway on the back side of the building.

"Where's the hotel gone?" he asked.

"I was hoping you'd tell me."

"You think I did this? No way. It's hard enough making dogs bark at a distance."

"Then who?"

Perkins shrugged. "I don't know. Listen, you should have a word with Tiger. He was trying to fool me into thinking that Patrick, Moobin, and the Prices have all been arrested, and he really shouldn't joke about that."

I raised an eyebrow and stared at him.

"Crumbs. You mean he wasn't kidding?"

"I wish he was."

I pressed the doorbell again, and a few minutes later Tiger answered. I explained what had happened, and after checking the other entrances and the windows — with one of us holding the front door open so we could get back in — we found that all access points led to an instant exit on the opposite side of the building. We couldn't agree who might have done it but did agree that it was an excellent defense — tested twenty minutes later when Villiers and Norton returned to "interview" Lady Mawgon. I shouted through the locked door that she would be surrendering herself to the authorities on Monday, and after a brief exchange of discourtesies, they left.

"Right," I said once I'd found my car keys. "I'm off to get help."

"What can I do?" asked Perkins.

"Help Tiger find out what you can about Blix. There must be something we can use to our advantage. Oh, and congratulations. You're doing the bridge gig on your own tomorrow."

He stared at me with a look of horror. "If I'm going to fail, I guess I should do it in a spectacular fashion."

I told him it wasn't over until it was over, went to my car, and was soon heading out of town.

FIFTEEN

Mother Zenobia

As I drove to Clifford to see Mother Zenobia, I wasn't very hopeful that I would have much luck recruiting her to our cause. She was old and tired and would turn herself to limestone for almost seventy percent of the day. What wizidrical powers she had available were most likely limited, and I knew for a fact that she hadn't been out of the convent for years. But I wasn't the only person who wanted to see Mother Zenobia that afternoon, and the presence of the other was neither welcome nor surprising.

It was none other than Conrad Blix, and I met him walking out of the Convent of the Blessed Ladies of the Lobster as I was walking in.

"Jennifer!" he said in a mockingly pleasant demeanor. "How is the team bearing up?"

"You know well enough," I replied coldly. "What are you doing here?"

He leaned closer. "Dealing with a few flies in this particular ointment, Miss Strange. This morning Villiers and Norton were merely assuring our victory. Just now I was guaranteeing it."

I didn't like the sound of this. "What have you done to her?"

He smiled. "I will get so much satisfaction watching you work for me as a parlor maid for the next two years. And for your complete and utter humiliation, I will *insist* you wear the uniform."

"You're a coward to use such underhanded means to win the most noble of contests, Blix."

He narrowed his eyes. "And you're very impertinent, considering you're nothing but a foundling who lucked out in your work assignment."

"On the contrary," I replied evenly. "Foundlings are *always* impertinent — it's because we have nothing to lose. I'm actually one of the politer ones."

"You'll regret your words, Jennifer."

"And you your actions," I replied. "And even if you do win, none of us will ever work for you."

"I wouldn't expect you to," he said. "All I need is

control of Kazam and, with it, a monopoly on magic—surely that's obvious?"

"To reanimate the mobile phone network?"

He grinned. "That's just for starters. You have no idea how much a wise investor can make by exploiting the crackle. The licensing deals on electromagical devices will earn a fortune—millions alone for something as simple as a pocket calculator. And all that work you're doing to reanimate medical scanners for *free*—deluded. How much do you think people will *pay* to detect an early tumor?"

I clenched and unclenched my fists. "Magic is not for the one," I said through gritted teeth. "It's for the many."

"I agree wholeheartedly. But in this particular instance, *many* means only myself, Lord Tenbury, the king, and his Useless Brother. Oh, and good move with Zambini Towers and the Infinite Thinness enchantment. Lady Mawgon, was it?" He didn't know she was stone, which was a small plus in our favor.

"She's very talented, if a little severe. We'll defeat you tomorrow, have no fear of that."

He laughed. "With who? A cranky washed-up old has-been and a winsome newbie who can barely levitate a brick? No. You'll be thrashed. Why don't you concede now and save the magic industry a lot of embarrassment?"

"The future of magic is not negotiable."

"You're wrong, and what's more, it's not your decision to make. Here's the deal for you to take back to Kazam: Concede before midnight tonight, and I will ensure that all those hopeless ex-sorcerers at Zambini — I mean, 'all those venerable past masters' — are looked after in a five-star nursing home until they croak. I will offer every licensed practitioner a choice: a job under my leadership or two million moolah cash in return for surrendering their magic licenses. What's more, you and Tiger will be paid to do nothing until your indentured servitude is finished, at which point you will be granted full citizenship. Do we have a deal?"

"Go to hell."

"Almost certainly," Blix replied with a smile, "but I'll go there wealthy. I'll expect an answer by midnight, yes?" His smile was smug and triumphant, but something didn't quite ring true.

"That's a very generous offer," I said, "for someone so utterly sure he will win. If you can thrash us like you claim, you can just take what you want from the wreckage without spending a bean. Why the offer? Do we *worry* you, Blix?"

He smiled again but not with quite so much confidence.

"Let's just say," Blix said, recovering his composure, "that the magic industry has enough bad PR without petty infighting. If we're to start selling magic as a benevolent force for good, as essential to daily life as the water in the tap and electricity in the wall, then we need to show we are responsible and upright citizens. Take the offer, Strange."

I had no intention of accepting his offer. "We'll see you at the bridge site tomorrow morning for the contest. Nine on the dot, wasn't it?"

"Nine it is. *Sandop kale n'baaa,* Miss Strange."

"*Sandop kale n'baaa,* Amazing Blix."

After staring at me for a moment, he turned on his heel and left.

I walked into the convent and soon found what Blix had been up to. Mother Zenobia was sitting in her chair, stony features looking straight ahead. She had changed to stone for her afternoon nap, and Blix, presumably, had blocked her return. I was too late. Blix had won this round, too. I took a deep breath and prepared to leave.

"Is there anything I can do?" asked a tearful Sister Agrippa, Mother Zenobia's attendant.

"Put a sheet over her and give her a once-over with a feather duster every two weeks. Don't use a vacuum cleaner in case you knock something off—she'd never forgive you when we get her back."

I walked out of the convent with the realization that the contest was as good as lost. With one potential sorcerer crossed off my list, my last hope was a woman who had won an unprecedented six golds in the sorcery events at the 1974 Olympics. She was a sorcerer of undisputed skills, but also secretive, obstinate, and prickly beyond measure.

She was the Once Magnificent Boo.

SIXTEEN

Boo and the Quarkbeasts

You couldn't work in the magic industry without knowing something about the Once Magnificent Boo. Today she was known chiefly as the magic license adjudicator, but she could have been much, much more. Miss Boolean Champernowne Waseed Mitford Smith had been an infant magic prodigy. At the age of five she was writing her own spells, was deemed Amazing by her tenth birthday, Incredible by her fifteenth, and Magnificent by the time she turned twenty. Her theory on Spell Entanglement for Multitasking was one of her most brilliant contributions, allowing for several enchantments to be done at the same time, a problem unsolved since the twelfth century. In short, she was doing stuff in her teens that the Mighty Shandar couldn't perform until he was in his thirties, and had been set to become the Next Great Thing — a sorcerer of astonishing powers, the type that crops up only every half millennia or so and changes the craft in new and exciting ways.

She never fulfilled that early promise, and not through her own fault. She was kidnapped in 1974 by anti-magic extremists; she hadn't done any magic since her release and rarely socialized with those who did. No one knew quite why, nor did she ever greet anyone with anything but a damp, stony silence when asked. But she hadn't totally forgotten her roots and, by way of the respect accorded to her, carried the Once Magnificent accolade.

Years after her kidnapping she was still in Hereford. In addition to her roles as an adjudicator and Beastmaster to the crown, she was also running the only rescue center for Quarkbeasts in the Northern Hemisphere. This was in Yarsop, a small village just off the Great West Road that led to the border with the Duchy of Brecon, and that's where I ended up a short drive later.

The Once Magnificent Boo's house was unremarkable; I had to check the address. Sorcerers usually lived in eccentrically built thatched hovels, full of junk and with owls and stuff hanging around outside. Not this house, one of a pair at the end of a gravel driveway, with weeping willows and flower beds neatly laid out. It was a picture of unmystical normality. I opened the gate and crunched down the path.

I pressed the doorbell and Once Magnificent Boo answered. Her white hair was tied back more neatly than when I'd seen her at the castle, but her eyes were still as dark as pitch, and I shivered as a cold rush of air escaped from the house. She still wore the gloves. She took one look at me, snorted, and shut the door in my face.

I didn't leave. It didn't make any sense to ring again now that she knew I was there, so I simply waited. Eight minutes ticked past and eventually the door opened.

"There's no business for you here, Miss Strange."

I took a deep breath. "A Quarkbeast once chose me for companionship."

"Yes, and your reckless custodianship led to its death."

This was true, and something that had preyed on my conscience these past two months. It had been a risky time in my life, and I'd made no effort to stop the Quarkbeast from following me into danger.

"For which I will never cease to be ashamed," I said softly. "I miss him greatly. Did you hear that a wild Quarkbeast was wandering around Hereford recently?"

"The colonel was here," she said shortly, "asking questions about how to trap one."

I told her about his plans for Quarkbeast-hunting

holiday trips for people with a lot more money than sense—and about Blix's involvement.

"They have no idea what they're meddling with," said Boo.

"Is there a way to stop him?" I asked.

She narrowed her eyes, thought for a moment, and then opened the door wide. "Come in, but be warned: Ask me to help you by doing some *m*-word, and I'll punch you in the eye. Understand?"

"Yes."

I stepped in. There was hardly any evidence at all of her past life as potentially one of the all-time greatest sorcerers ever. From her home I could see only that she was obsessed with Quarkbeasts to a degree that was probably unhealthy, played croquet for the county, and liked to cross-stitch cushions.

"Nice place," I said.

"Adequate for my needs," she replied, seemingly less unfriendly now that we were in her house. "Which Quarkbeast was yours?"

I took a picture from my shoulder bag and showed her. "The photographer was trembling with fear when he took it," I explained, "so it's a bit blurred."

"Hmm," said Once Magnificent Boo as she took the picture to a desk and opened a book full of Quarkbeast illustrations. This wasn't just a rescue center, I realized;

she was studying them. She pulled out a picture and showed it to me.

"Was that yours?"

I stared carefully. "No."

She turned to the large Florentine mirror above the mantel and held up the picture so I could see it in mirror image—and I felt a tear spring to my eye with the sudden recognition.

"That's him."

"Not him, *it*," corrected Once Magnificent Boo, scribbling in a notepad. "Quarkbeasts are genderless. You had Q27. Now, is this the beast you saw in town?" She held up the photograph I carried of my own Quarkbeast so it was reflected in the mirror.

"Yes, the one I saw just yesterday."

"Then we've got the match of your Quarkbeast sniffing around—Q28. It took it two months to get here from Australia, which was to be expected. Quarkbeasts aren't strong swimmers."

"It swam twelve thousand miles?"

"Don't be ridiculous. It swam *eight* thousand miles— the rest would have been on land at a fast trot."

"That's quite a migration."

"Quarks are remarkable beasts. Do you want to see some?"

"Yes, please."

We walked out the back door, which I noted had

been broken recently and crudely repaired, and into a paddock at the back, where four Quarkbeasts were happily sunning themselves.

"Quark," said the one closest to me.

"Quark," said another.

"Quark," said the third.

"Quark," came the muffled call of one from inside the pen.

It was quite an emotional moment. Although each call was subtly different and none of the beasts looked like mine, each looked like it *might* be, which was a bit odd and unnerving.

"That's Q3," said Boo, pointing to a mangy-looking specimen missing most of its back plates. "I rescued it from a Quark-baiting ring. A very cruel sport. Over there is Q11, which got run over on the highway and was dragged for six miles. You can still see the eight grooves its claws made in the road all the way from the Premier Inn to the Newent exit. Q35 is the one lying in the wallow of iron filings. It was captured alive in the jam and biscuit section of the Holmer Road Co-op. The beast with the missing teeth is Q23. I got it from the zoo after they thought it was frightening the public too much. I had them all registered as dangerous pets. Legally, no one can touch them — not even the colonel."

She looked at me for a moment, then opened a cardboard box full of dog food tins. With a gloved hand she tossed them toward the Quarkbeasts, who crunched them up eagerly, tin and all.

"What do the neighbors think about having them here?" I asked. The four looked so fearsome that only those well acquainted with the species would be relaxed around them.

"They're okay about it—they think it keeps burglars away. It doesn't." She indicated the damaged back door. "Last Tuesday night. Did the beasts let out a single Quark? Not one."

"Take much?" I asked, stalling as I tried to figure out a way to raise the "Can you help us?" issue without getting punched in the eye.

"Money, jewelry, that kind of stuff. I thought of leaving a Quarkbeast in the house at night, but, well, there are some things you balk at doing, even to burglars."

She was right. No one deserves a savaging by a Quarkbeast—or even being surprised by one when off doing some innocent villainy.

"Do they like it here?"

"They *seem* happy, but since they're running on Mandrake Sentience Emulation Protocols to make us think they're real, we can't ever know for sure."

"So what is Q28 doing in town?" I asked. "If its twin is dead, it can't be looking for him, surely?"

The Once Magnificent Boo stared at me intently. "Are you ready to be confused?"

"It's how I spend most of my days at Zambini Towers."

"Then here it is: Quarkbeasts breed by creating an exact mirror copy of themselves—and since the Mighty Shandar created only one Quarkbeast, every Quarkbeast is a copy of every other Quarkbeast, only opposite."

"I was blown backwards yesterday," I said. "Is that the same thing?"

"No, and if I were you, I would stay that way. It will save your life."

"Right. But wait a minute." I looked at the picture of Q26, the one that paired to produce mine. "If Q27 is the mirror of Q26 and Q28 is the mirror of Q27, then why don't Q26 and Q28 look the same? Aren't alternate generations identical?"

"No. It's more complicated than that. They create identical copies of themselves in six different flavors: *Up, Down, Charm, Strange, Top,* and *Bottom.* All are opposite and equal, but all uniquely different and alike at the same time."

"I don't understand any of this."

"I have problems with it still, after twenty years," confessed Boo. "The complexities of the Quarkbeast are fundamentally unknowable. But here's the point: There can only ever be thirty-six completely unique yet identical Quarkbeasts. If they divide in such a way that all the combinations are fulfilled, they will come together and merge into a single quota of fully quorumed Quark-beasts."

"What will happen then?"

"Something *wonderful*. All the great unanswered questions of the world will be answered. Who are we? What are we here for? Where will we end up? And most important of all: Can mankind actually get any stupider? The Quarkbeast is more than an animal; it's an oracle. It assists in mankind's elusive search for meaning, truth, and fulfillment."

"Really?"

"Don't take my word for it. It was foreseen by Sister Yolanda of Kilpeck."

Yolanda was a good pre-cog. If she said enlighten-ment would be attained when there was a full thirty-six Quarkbeast quota, there was a good chance it would.

"When will this happen?"

"Good question. The last near quota was two months ago. For eight minutes there were thirty-four Quark-beasts in existence; if two had divided, the full thirty-six would have been accomplished. When yours died the to-tal dropped to thirty-three. By the end of the week there were twenty-nine on the planet. We're down to fifteen at the moment. Poaching is increasing, and the colonel and his type need to be stopped. Quarkbeasts shouldn't be messed around with, and they should never be held against their will. Can I rely on you to do what you can to ensure it remains free?"

"Of course." I suddenly had a realization. "They use magic to copy themselves, don't they?"

"You learn quick," Boo replied. "They do, but since they require a whopping one-point-two gigashandars for a successful separation, they can't do it alone. They need a sorcerer of considerable power to channel the energy. They can store power, too, just like fireflies — but unlike fireflies, who transmit the power out as light immediately, Quarks can store it for a day or two."

"Patrick surged yesterday. There was a Quarkbeast close by."

"Pat's a sweet man, but he doesn't have the skill to channel that amount of power. Since Zambini vanished, no one does. Quark division is unlikely, but if it happens, it creates a very dangerous situation. See that vehicle over there?" She pointed to a riveted titanium box about the size of small garden shed, mounted on the back of a rusty E-Type Jaguar fitted with blue lights and sirens.

"Yes?"

"If Quarkbeasts divide, they must be separated within a thousand seconds or they may merge again, with devastating results," said Boo. "I'm the kingdom's Beastcatcher, so I have full emergency vehicle status. If you think a pair are about to conjoin, call 999 and yell

'Quarkbeast' in a panicked, half-strangled cry of terror. They'll put you straight through."

I took a deep breath. Much as I wanted to know more about Quarkbeasts, it was now or never. I looked behind me to make sure there were no sharp objects close by.

"What are you doing?" asked Boo.

"I'm going to ask you something and you're going to punch me, and I wanted to make sure I don't hurt myself on the way down."

She gave me an inky-black glare, and a coldness suddenly washed around me as though someone had opened a tomb. I closed my eyes.

"I need help," I said. "Magic is in dire straits."

I winced, expecting the blow to fall. After a few seconds I opened my eyes to find that Once Magnificent Boo had walked away. She was dropping a gearbox from a truck into the beasts' compound, where they would gnaw off the soft aluminum casing and use the harder cogs for nesting.

"Magic is *always* in dire straits," said Boo. "It's the nature of magic. But that part of my life has finished. I can do nothing for you. I haven't committed a single spell since the anti-magic extremists dumped me in that roadside rest area many years ago."

"But Blix wants to control Kazam and commercialize magic," I pleaded. "We can't let it happen."

She took several steps closer, and I backed away until

I was pressed against a water spigot. She looked at me with her empty eyes and spoke in a low voice that seemed to reverberate inside my head.

"And who's better qualified to decide what's best for magic? Blix or Zambini?"

"Zambini."

"Are you sure? The right way, the wrong way — it's all regulation. Maybe magic shouldn't be regulated at all. Maybe it should take its own path, like the Quarkbeast, unfettered by our meddling. Perhaps magic needs to be used for evil before it can take the right course for good, and if so, Zambini's need to control it is as damaging as Blix. The only thing that separates the pair of them is their viewpoint and dress sense."

This was true. Zambini was a shabby dresser, and Blix was always well turned out.

"With respect, you're wrong," I said. "Zambini's nothing like Blix. He's kind and good and honest and —"

"Missing?"

"Okay, yes, but Blix is no friend to the right and true direction of magic, and I need help to defeat him."

She took another step toward me. She was now so close that I could feel her breath on my face and see every detail on hers, from the fine capillaries in her eyes to the broken blood vessels on the side of her nose. Her eyes were very black, as if she had massive pupils and no irises at all.

"I can't help you. I can't help *anyone* anymore."

"Is there nothing I can do or say to persuade you to help us?"

"Nothing."

The Once Magnificent Boo turned back to the Quarkbeasts and continued to feed them, so I thanked her, said my goodbyes, and returned to my car.

I drove back into town in a despondent mood. I was disappointed but not surprised that Boo had rejected my request. We had no hope of winning the contest. I would have to think very carefully about either taking Blix's offer to concede or coming up with another plan—and quickly.

And that was when a large black Daimler four-by-four with tinted windows pulled in front of me. I stamped heavily on the brakes and skidded to a halt.

SEVENTEEN

The North Tower

I slammed the Volkswagen into reverse as another Daimler screeched to a halt behind me. I opened the car door and tried to jump out, but in my hurry I forgot to unbuckle my seat belt. I was still struggling to extricate myself when four huge bodyguards dragged me out of my car, put a hood over my head and cuffs on my wrists, and threw me into the back of the first Daimler.

"Don't hurt me," I said from the floor as the car sped off.

"Then be a good girl and don't struggle," came a patronizing voice.

"It's not for my benefit," I told them. "It's for yours.

If I lose my temper, those of you still conscious in two minutes will be picking up the teeth of those who aren't."

There was a pause, and I was then picked up and placed on a seat.

"Comfy?" came the voice, this time tinged with a little respect. It seemed they had been warned not to underestimate me.

"Yes, thank you."

"Cuffs not too tight?"

"No, they're fine."

"Sure?"

"Yes, really," I said in a sweet voice, just to unnerve him. "You're most kind."

The journey was not long, and from the sounds of creaking drawbridges and tires on cobbled roads, it didn't take a genius to figure out where I was being taken. After a short time the car stopped and I was carried up a long flight of steps. I was then laid on a soft bed before I heard some footsteps hurry away, a door slam, a lock turn, and then more hurried steps down a stone staircase followed by another door slamming, another lock turning, and then the whole thing repeating itself until I could no longer hear it.

After a few seconds my bonds and hood melted away to nothing. Proof, as if any had been needed, of Blix's involvement.

As I expected, I was in the High North Tower of

the king's castle at Snodd Hill. It was comfortable, if a bit austere in the same medieval dreary chic style of the King's Useless Brother's office. The large pile of provisions and bottled water clearly meant that I was to be here for some time — or at least until after the bridge contest.

I tried the door and found it firmly locked, then looked out the window. The High North Tower had been accurately if unimaginatively named, being a tower, to the north, and, most pertinent to me, high. The room was circular and barely twenty feet across and sat precariously atop a long and mildly off-kilter column of crumbling stonework.

I wasn't going to escape from here without a lot of help. The room was clearly meant to be a long-term prison of some comfort — there was a large and cushy-looking bed, a bureau, a kitchenette, and even a well-appointed bathroom and a telephone. I didn't think there would be room service, though.

After almost two hours, the phone rang. I could guess who it was.

"Hello, Blix," I said before he could say anything. "Adding kidnapping to your long list of felonies?"

"We prefer to think of it as 'vacationing at the specific invitation of His Majesty,'" replied Blix. "Open the top drawer of the bureau."

I did so, and found a contract for Kazam to concede

the competition, with all the details that Blix had already outlined. The document had been prepared by a law firm in Financia and registered with the Ununited Kingdoms Supreme Court, so even if King Snodd had wanted to reverse the deal, he couldn't.

"It's all there," said Blix. "I knew my or the king's word would not be good enough, so I made it official. Sign it and your vacation in the North Tower is over."

"And if I don't?"

"Then you'll stay there until six Mondays from now, and we'll have Kazam for nothing."

"Blix?"

"Yes?"

"Are you in the castle watching the top of the North Tower at the moment?"

"I might be."

I ripped the phone from the wall and tossed it out the open window. The telephone took almost five seconds to hit the ground. It was a pointless gesture, but very satisfying. I was trying to mask my feelings of helplessness with hubris, but I was kidding myself.

Dejected, I went and sat on the bed, glad for quiet time to think. Oddly enough, the one thing that gave me any confidence that we'd win the contest was the fact that Blix was still nervous enough to want to do deals. I went over the events of the past few days, attempting to find something that might help us. What had I missed? The answer *had* to be there.

I was stirred from my thoughts by the wail of an air-raid siren and the unmistakable *crack* of an artillery piece close by. I looked out the window as the massed antiaircraft defenses of Snodd opened up as one, a cacophony so loud I put my hands over my ears. The shells were bursting so close that I could hear shrapnel striking the tower. A piece of red-hot steel flew in the window and landed on the bed, where it began to smolder; I used my handkerchief to pick it up and dumped it into the sink.

I ventured another look out. Amid the din, smell of cordite, and black bursts of flak that were drifting past my window, I saw something shoot past, the flak bursts following it. That the kingdom was under attack was unlikely, as the king currently had no enemies interested enough to attack him. It was only when my name was called that I realized what was going on.

"Jenny!" Prince Nasil whipped past on his carpet. "Can't stop!" he added as he sped back in the opposite direction, then yelled "Jump!" as he tore past the third time, two antiaircraft shells exploding so close that the tower shook and plaster fell from the ceiling.

I needed no further bidding. I shoved Blix's contract into my bag, waited until the prince turned to make another pass, and then jumped out the window.

I'd never fallen from a high tower before and hope never to do so again, but after the initial fear and rapid acceleration, all I could feel was the air rushing past me. I could see the top of the tower move swiftly away, and didn't see the prince at all until he gently scooped me out of the air. With a flick of the carpet we were out of the range of the artillery, which stopped as quickly as it had begun.

"Thanks for the rescue," I said, "but it might have been easier and safer to extract me at night."

"At night?" echoed the prince. "If we'd left it until then, there would be no chance of seeing Zambini."

The penny dropped. "Kevin knows *where* the Great Zambini is going to reappear?"

"Not precisely — but close enough. Somewhere near the Troll Wall."

My heart fell. "The Troll Wall is almost fifty miles long!"

"If we head up there now, we can home in when Kevin has a more accurate fix."

This was undoubtedly true, as Kevin's predictions of Zambini's return had been uncannily accurate — just too late to be of any real use. I looked at my watch. We had less than an hour to go before Zambini was due back.

"We'll never make it," I said as we flew through the ballroom windows at Zambini Towers and slid to a halt on the shiny floor.

"We have a plan," said the prince, and I looked up. Perkins, Owen of Rhayder, Kevin Zipp, and Tiger were all staring at me.

"I'm all ears," I said as Tiger handed me two sweaters, some thermal leggings, a heavy leather flying jacket, and a flying helmet.

"It's a straight-line flight of two hundred and eighty miles to the Troll Gates at Stirling," said Owen, referring to a blackboard upon which a diagram had been hastily drawn, "and if we leave in five minutes, we have thirty-two minutes to get there. That's an average speed requirement of five hundred and twenty-five miles per hour."

I saw the problem. "Even by moving at the carpet's top design speed of five hundred miles per hour," I murmured, "we would still be . . . two and a half minutes too late."

But Owen and the prince were ahead of the curve.

"*Precisely,*" said the prince. "That's why we need to push the carpets to over seven hundred and sixty miles per hour during the flight to give us any hope of getting there in time."

I looked at them both in turn. "You intend to go *supersonic?*"

"Trust us," said Owen with a smile. "It's faintly possible that we know what we're doing. Get prepared. We'll be rugging off in two minutes."

Owen and the prince went to rewrite a few lines of the carpet's source spell code, and I turned back to Tiger and Perkins.

"You'll be out of range for a baby shoe, so we're going to conch," Perkins said. He held a pair of left- and right-handed conches together for a moment, whispered a spell, and then gave one shell to me.

"Can you hear me?" His voice echoed out of the shell, clear as a bell. In fact, I heard him slightly *before* he spoke, which caused an odd reverse echo.

"How did it go with Once Magnificent Boo?" asked Tiger.

"Not well; she doesn't want to help us. And she wouldn't say why she stopped doing any magic, but it sounded like something pretty unpleasant."

"It figures that she knew Zambini and Blix well," said Tiger as he showed me a photograph. "They were all on the UnUK Olympic sorcery team in 1974."

It looked like Tiger's research had paid off. The photo showed the three of them much younger, posing after winning gold for the prestigious 400 Meters Turning into a Mouse Relay event. Boo was grinning broadly, with Blix and Zambini on either side of her. Unlike Boo's, their smiles looked somewhat strained.

"They were the best of friends," said Tiger, "and inseparable until Boo was kidnapped. Zambini was away when it happened, so Blix negotiated the ransom. Then

Blix and Zambini fought big-time, and they've been at each other's throats ever since. That's about it."

"History of petty infighting doesn't help us," I said with a sigh. "Did you find out where the Infinite Thinness enchantment was coming from?"

"Not yet, but the spell's holding up well. Blix's sorcerers have been out there attempting to get into Zambini Towers all afternoon, but no matter how much power they use to attempt to break the enchantment, the spell uses even more to stop them."

"Let's hope it stays that way," I said, digging Blix's conceding document from my bag and handing it to Perkins. "As acting senior wizard, you can sign this without my consent," I told him, and explained exactly what it was. "You should ask the retired sorcerers, too. I can't make this decision alone, and what's more, I shouldn't have to. We've got until midnight tonight. Nothing on Lady Mawgon or the passthought, I presume?"

"Nothing," said Perkins, "except the Dibbles are at full capacity and occasionally venting into the atmosphere."

"I saw the cloud shapes as we flew over."

Perkins's eyes opened wide as he read the document. "Two million moolah if I agree never to spell again?"

"All that moolah must be worth a fortune," remarked Tiger.

I looked at the prince, who nodded that they were ready. This was it.

"If I don't make it back," I said to Tiger, "you're to take over as acting manager in my place."

He gave me a hug. Perkins looked as though he wanted to and said, "Break a leg."

I walked over to where Owen and the prince were making last-minute adjustments to the hemp backing of Owen's carpet. "You're sure about this?" I asked.

"Not at all," said Owen as he handed the prince and me each a parachute while he strapped one on himself, "but we need the Great Zambini back, and this is the best chance we've had so far."

"Then what are we waiting for?" I asked, giving them both a nervous smile.

I put on all the garb Tiger had handed me and added the parachute, with Tiger's help, then stepped onto the front of the carpet, sat cross-legged, and pulled the goggles down over my eyes. The prince jumped onto the back, raised the carpet into a hover, turned it around, and sped out the open windows with Owen in close formation behind. I caught just a glimpse of the many assorted police cars and military vehicles that had surrounded Zambini Towers before we were off and away, heading for Trollvania.

EIGHTEEN

Mach 1.02

A s we headed off to the northwest, I examined the state of Prince Nasil's carpet: old and threadbare. It needed a complete overhaul, but since the chief component necessary for flight was angel feathers and these were as rare as hen's teeth—coincidentally *also* one of the components—then replacing his or Owen's carpets anytime soon was just shy of impossible. There was little to do except fly them sparingly until they could fly no more.

I can't say I've ever really felt at ease traveling by carpet, partly because of the ropey state of the rug and partly because one feels so very exposed. It's not possible to fall off due to the RugStuck enchantment that clamps passengers and operators to the weave, but the rush of air is highly disconcerting, which is why carpets rarely go above twice the speed of horse. It's just too cold. Besides, if you have to do pizza deliveries, it cools them down too fast and everyone complains.

We climbed to our higher-than-normal operating height of five thousand feet, with Owen of Rhayder stationed less than ten feet away. Pretty soon we were over the verdant countryside of the Kingdom of Shropshire, and once clear of built-up areas, we prepared for the jump to supersonic. The prince told me to lie flat, then joined me as the front of the carpet folded up in a curve in front of us with the ragged hem now level with our shoulders. It would keep the worst of the wind from us, make the carpet more aerodynamic, and provide more safety. Striking a bee at transonic speeds could take out an eye — and ruin a bee's day, too.

Owen then maneuvered in behind us as we zipped along, and the hem on the front of his carpet intertwined with the rear of ours, making one long carpet. After Owen and Nasil gave each other a thumbs-up, they hunkered down in a crouch to reduce drag. Both carpets started to accelerate rapidly.

I have been on wild rides before and since, but nothing can compare with that flight up to the Troll Wall. It would have been, in fact, a world speed record if we'd cared to have it ratified, but those thoughts weren't really on our minds.

"We have to use Owen's carpet to accelerate us up to six hundred and fifty!" shouted the prince as the wispy clouds whipped past faster and faster. "After that, we're on our own!"

I have to admit that I was scared. As Nasil yelled, "Four hundred!" the rug began to vibrate in a most disturbing manner, but this was nothing compared with the bucking and twisting that occurred at five hundred, and soon we were shaking so much, it was hard to focus on the lakes, rivers, trees, and houses that shot past beneath us.

"Six hundred!" yelled the prince, and I twisted around to look at Owen lying flat on his carpet, waiting for the signal. As his old, worn carpet pushed us well beyond its design speed, the weave and weft started to separate with the strain—and at just under 620 miles per hour, a hole opened up. In an instant the air caught it and the carpet was gone in a burst of tattered wool and cotton. The hem released, and Owen, his part of the job complete, was tossed into the void. We watched him fall away, his body splayed out to decelerate enough so he could safely deploy his parachute. We breathed a sigh of relief when we saw his canopy blossom open somewhere over Midlandia, and I felt Prince Nasil's body tense as he urged his carpet on.

The carpet was still vibrating badly, and I saw small holes appear where the weave was already badly worn. I had just shut my eyes and moved my hand to the D-ring of my parachute when there was a muffled blast somewhere in the far distance. Everything suddenly went smooth. I looked out. On either side of us were shock waves barely a yard wide that trailed from the front edges of the carpet, which had folded back into a V like a paper airplane. I turned to Nasil, but he was concentrating hard, and we continued at this pace for several minutes. With every passing second, the carpet showed more wear.

I had my eyes shut tight as soon as the vibrations began again, and I had just resigned myself to my second free fall that day when I realized that we weren't breaking up but decelerating. A few minutes later we were flying slowly along the First Troll Wall. My extraordinary relief made me want to hug the prince, but royal protocol disallowed it, so I simply smiled and congratulated him.

"Do you think Owen's okay?" I asked.

"I saw his parachute open."

"Me, too. What about your carpet?"

Large sections had peeled off and were flapping in the breeze. He shook his head sadly.

"We'll take longer to get home, Jennifer, my friend, and she'll not be flying until a rebuild."

"Then let's hope Zambini's close by."

The Troll Wall was a vast stone edifice more than three hundred feet high and topped with rusty spikes. The Second Troll Wall was located about ten miles farther north, the result of a foolish misunderstanding three centuries earlier about which wizard had been allocated the building contract. It hadn't made much difference. One wall or two, the trolls still made meat patties of anyone who crossed over. The two walls stretched from Clyde in the west and then clear across the country to Stirling in the east.

We approached and then circled the City of Stirling, where the Troll Gates — a pair of oak doors seventy feet high and strengthened with steel bands — were located. The last Troll War had been twelve years before, and after repairs and a lock change on the Troll Gates, everything had pretty much returned to normal, except that human settlers in the zone between the two walls had been moved out "just in case."

"Jennifer?" came Tiger's voice over the conch.

I told Tiger we were at Stirling and looked at my watch. We had three minutes before Zambini was due to reappear.

"Okay," said Tiger. "Kevin's not sure, but he thinks you're to head to an abandoned village called Kippen, about eight miles west of the main gates and four miles north of the First Troll Wall."

I relayed the information to Nasil, who whirled his carpet around. We shot off in that direction, skimming along the top of the wall as fast as the tattered state of the carpet would allow.

"See any trolls?" asked Nasil as we crossed the first wall and went into what was now deemed unfriendly territory.

"What does one look like?" I asked. Few people had seen one and survived.

"Large, and usually covered in tattoos and war paint. Clubs and axes are optional."

"We'll know when we see one, I guess." Even looking hard I could see no sign of life — just an empty landscape showing that people had once lived here. We saw a few abandoned landships encrusted with ivy as we headed west, their rusty flanks suggesting they'd burned first.

After another few minutes the remains of a long-abandoned town came into sight, and a quick look at the road sign on the outskirts told us we were indeed in Kippen. The prince started to orbit slowly as I checked my watch. It was 3:59 and 14 seconds.

We had made it with four minutes to spare.

NINETEEN

Trollvania

That will be my landing zone," said the prince, pointing at an open area of scrubby land behind the village church. "I'll drop you off and then orbit until you signal me in for evacuation."

"Don't come and get me until I call you," I said, "no matter what. If I'm longer than half an hour, I'm not returning; tell Tiger he can have my record collection and Volkswagen. Understand?"

"I understand. Good luck."

"Thank you."

I looked around nervously as we approached low across a heavily overgrown neighborhood, half expecting a troll to jump out at any moment. Trolls are noted for two things: their ability to hide motionless and undetected in a damp riverbed or pile of dead wood for months if necessary, and a lack of any sense of moderation when it comes to the use of violence. An arm pulled from its socket was generally just a start, and it tended to get more unpleasant from there on in.

The prince stopped the carpet a few feet from the ground, and I jumped off. In an instant he was gone again and I was alone. I stood there for a moment, looking around. After the noisy rush of air on our journey north, all was now deathly quiet. Around me, the remains of houses were partially reclaimed by a healthy growth of trees, brambles, and moss. I could see the church's damaged tower, the clock stuck permanently at ten to four. To my right was a rusty landship, apparently now a home only to ravens. There was no sign of Mr. Zambini, trolls, or any life at all, so I pulled off my parachute, flying helmet, and bulky jacket and dumped them onto the grass. I made sure my flare pistol was loaded and placed the conch close to my lips.

"Tiger?" I whispered as I climbed over the wall at the back of the church. "Are you there?"

"I'm here," he said. "Kevin's gone into a trance and is mumbling. Is that good news?"

"Usually."

"Good. Hang on, he's saying something." There was

a pause. "Okay, here it is: *The monument at Four Roads.* Make any sense?"

"Not yet," I replied, "but knowing Kevin, it soon will."

As my ears gradually stopped ringing from the flight, I could hear rustles and creaks from the abandoned village, which made me more apprehensive. I walked up the road, which had weeds growing out of large cracks, and passed a rusty bicycle, scattered bricks, and broken tiles. There was evidence of fierce fighting, too. Lying in the dirt were the occasional corroded weapon, sections of body armor, and human bones, some of which looked as though they had been cracked to extract the marrow.

"Okay," I said to Tiger, "I'm at the top of Fore Street, where there is a crossroads and the remains of a stone monument."

"Close enough. I think you're there," he replied over the conch.

I looked around at the empty, shattered town. Towering above the crossroads was the abandoned landship I had seen from behind the church. It had halted atop the rubble of some houses opposite the monument, its twenty-foot-wide tracks sitting on a rusty ice cream truck.

It was 4:03 and 14 seconds precisely, and the Great Zambini was nowhere to be seen.

I yelled his name as loud as I could but regretted it. The sound echoed around the still village, and from somewhere in the distance I heard the breaking of roof tiles. Something had moved. Something big.

"I need some more help," I said into the conch. "Anything at all."

I hid behind the heavy tracks of the landship and peered cautiously out. Farther up the road I saw a large tree sway. There was another distant crash and the sound of breaking glass, and I caught a glimpse of something move between two houses. Then, from the direction of the church, I heard a low guttural cry and I froze.

There were two of them, and one had just found my flying jacket and parachute.

I felt myself break out into a sweat and pressed harder against the rusty tracks of the landship. I dug the flare pistol out of my bag in preparation. If I used it, the prince would fly in and pick me up—but that would also give away my position to the trolls. I'd have to hope he could move faster than they could.

I heard another crash and looked up to see a cloud of dust roll into the street. A few seconds later a troll stepped into the roadway. I like to think that not much frightens me, but trolls certainly did. This one was a muscular male about twenty-five feet tall, carrying a large club fashioned from the bough of an oak. It was dressed in a loincloth made of cowhides stitched together, and aside from a pair of sandals and a small leather skullcap onto which was stuck a juniper bush and a dried goat, it was naked. It seemed to have no body hair, and its face was smooth, with just two holes for nostrils, no chin to speak of, a large mouth with two tusks jutting up against its cheeks, and small eyes set deep into its skull. But what was most remarkable about the troll was that its body was covered in a swirling pattern of fine tattoos that made it look both utterly fearsome and curiously elegant.

The troll sniffed the air and then called out in a voice that sounded like the deepest of organ pipes. Another troll soon joined the first, absently removing a brick chimney on its way past and scrunching the bricks to powder in its massive fist.

"Is this from a human?" asked the second troll, holding out my flying jacket between finger and thumb the same way you might hold a week-old dead mouse. The jacket, while big and bulky on me, looked like dolls' clothes in the troll's enormous hand.

"Regretfully so," replied the first in a surprisingly elegant tone as he unclipped a bugle he wore at his waist. "I'll call pest control."

"Do we have to?" said the second troll, laying his hand on the first troll's forearm. "I know vermin have to be kept down, but one's not going to cause any trouble, surely?"

The first troll looked at his colleague reproachfully. "Don't get all sentimental, Hadridd. They're dirty, spread diseases, and breed *endlessly*. Did you know that a colony can outgrow the capacity of its environment in as little as twelve centuries? I know they look cute and can do tricks and make that funny squeaking noise when you stare at them close, but honestly, culling is really for their own good."

"We could keep it as a pet," said the second troll in a hopeful sort of voice. "Hagridd has two and says they're delightful."

"I've always thought keeping humans as pets was a bit disgusting," said the first with a shudder, "and if you let the children play with them, they inevitably get thrown around the garden, and that's just cruel. No, better to just snap their necks and be done with it."

"I suppose so," said the second troll, then added, "Shouldn't we make sure there's an infestation *before* we call pest control? You know what a state they get into over false alarms."

"You're right," said the first, and they sniffed at my jacket again, then began to walk in my direction.

"Not what you expect, are they?" came a familiar voice.

I turned, and there was the Great Zambini.

He was tall and handsome and was smiling in that fatherly manner that I had found so calming when I was new at Kazam. It was all I could do to stop myself from bursting into tears and flinging my arms around him.

"Thank heavens," I managed to say, swallowing down my emotions. "We haven't much time —"

"Then we won't waste it here, young lady." Mr. Zambini ushered me through a rusty ground-level escape hatch in the landship just as the trolls rounded the corner. "This way."

He led me past some machinery and up a steel staircase in the semi-gloom. As we reached the lower storage deck of the fighting vehicle, we heard the trolls outside.

"We'll *never* get it now," said one.

"I've an idea," said the other.

We heard them walk off, then some low murmurs.

"We're safe for the moment," said Zambini, leading me past the main engine room and up toward the B deck, where the crew quarters were located. "Their knowledge of humans is fairly rudimentary."

This particular landship had not been set on fire, and all the crew's provisions and equipment were still where they had been abandoned — food, water, and racks of weapons, all with the Snodd Heavy Industries logo on them. Zambini sat on a crew couch and stared at me.

"How long have I been gone?" he asked.

"Eight months."

He opened his eyes wide and shook his head sadly. "That long? This is my sixteenth return, and each runs into the next — it's like casting oneself into stone but without the splitting headache upon waking. We've got about six minutes, by the way — I can't stop myself from vanishing again, but I can delay it. However did you find me, and what's been going on?"

I told him quickly about Kevin, how we had to trash both the carpets to get up here in time, about the Big Magic, that we had two more dragons and wizidrical power was on the rise, and then how King Snodd made Blix the Court Mystician.

"Theoretically that makes Blix eighth in line to the throne," said Zambini, incredulous.

"It sounds as if the king and Tenbury are hell-bent on commercializing magic," I told him, "and they want to take control of Kazam. We've got a contest to decide the matter tomorrow."

"Kazam will win hands down," observed Zambini. "Blix and his cronies are useless."

"I'm not so sure. Lady Mawgon got changed to stone while trying to hack the Dibble Storage Coils, and all the others are in prison on trumped-up charges — which leaves only Perkins. We don't have a chance, unless you can tell us how to unlock the Dibbles. Please, you must help us. We've got four gigashandars of power sitting there doing nothing."

"Without a passthought, you can't, and the only

people who know RUNIX well enough to crack it are me, Mawgon, Monty Vanguard, and Blix. And I can't get back."

"Monty is stone, too, and I'm not keen on asking Blix for help."

Zambini smiled. "Blix as stone might solve a lot of problems."

"But what if he succeeds? I'm not sure handing him four gig of raw crackle is a good idea."

"I agree with you on that score."

And that was when we heard the trolls again.

"Here, person person person," came a deep voice from near the rear cargo door. "I've got some lovely yummy honey for you. Here, person person person." There was a pause. "Do you think it's gone?"

"No. Leave the honey there, and we'll S-Q-U-A-S-H the human when it comes to get it."

"Right."

All went quiet again.

"Anything else?" whispered Zambini, getting to his feet and pacing around the crew quarters.

"Anything else?" I echoed. "Does there need to be anything else? The future of magic is in the balance!"

"The thing about magic," said Zambini in a soft voice, "is that it often seems to have intelligence. It moves in the direction it wants to. It may decide to let iMagic win as part of some big mysterious plan to which we are not yet party. Or, if it thinks Kazam should win tomorrow, it will find a way to ensure that we do."

"I'm not sure how," I replied somewhat dubiously. "I even asked Once Magnificent Boo to help us."

Zambini looked up at me, genuine concern on his face. "How is she?"

"She lives alone with a lot of Quarkbeasts. A bit batty, if you ask me, and horribly selfish — she refused to help us."

"Do you know why she hasn't undertaken a single spell since her kidnapping?"

I shook my head.

Zambini paused and took a deep breath. "Ever wondered why she never shakes hands? Why she always wears gloves?"

I stared at him, and an awful realization welled up inside me.

"Yes," he said, holding up his own index fingers — the conduit of power, without which every sorcerer would be powerless. "She wasn't returned unharmed. *The kidnappers removed her index fingers.*"

I didn't speak for several moments. Boo could have been one of the all-time greats, and now she was studying Quarkbeasts and going slowly nuts. She lived with her loss every day, knowing that a life of wonder and fulfillment in the Mystical Arts had been cruelly taken from her. I couldn't imagine what it might be like. Greatness had slipped from her grasp.

"Who did it?"

"Two of the gang were found dead a week later, apparently over a squabble. There might have been others, but no trace was ever found. I was away in Italy talking to Fabio Spontini about his work on magical-field theory, and by the time I got back, they'd already taken her fingers. She blamed me for not being there, and Blix for messing up the negotiations."

"Did he?"

"I don't know, but I don't think he would have. We both loved her dearly, and the three of us could have done great things together—stuff that would have made the Mighty Shandar look like a Saturday-afternoon hobbyist. But then Boo lost her fingers, Blix and I fought over the direction of magic, and that was it. She's not talked to either of us since."

He sighed and looked at his watch. "Two minutes left. I need to give you something."

He reached into his pocket and pulled out an envelope covered with tiny writing. "This is a list of notes I've been making while I've been jumping around. For a while I thought my inability to return was an accident—that I'd misspelled while vanishing. But now that you've told me about the failure of Shandar to destroy the dragon two months ago, I'm beginning to think it might have been the Mighty Shandar himself who wanted me out of the picture during the Big Magic. And now he has unfinished business that will keep me trapped out here for as long as he wants, rattling around the here and now like a pea in a whistle."

"What sort of unfinished business?"

"This: He was paid eighteen dray-weights of gold to rid the Ununited Kingdoms of dragons. He failed, and the Mighty Shandar doesn't do refunds. He'll want to return and deal with the dragons once and for all. He'll also want to take his revenge on the person who helped the dragons foil his plan in the first place. Who was that, by the way?"

"Me."

"Oh, dear."

Zambini paced for a moment as he thought. He had done this when he was back at the Towers, and seeing him do it now made me miss him more than ever. I wanted him back. To make the decisions, to be the one in charge, to sometimes make the *wrong* decisions and ignore the criticism.

"You must be vigilant," he said at last. "The job of Shandar's agent has been filled by the D'Argento family for four centuries. They report to him when he comes out of granite for one minute every month. He'll leave the donkey work up to them and only appear himself for the seriously big spelling stuff, so you should know what to be wary of. His agent will be well spoken, well dressed, ride around in a midnight-black top-of-the-line Rolls-Royce, and have an anagrammatic name. A bit corny, I know, but it's traditional, apparently."

I covered my face with my hands. The young lady in the Phantom Twelve. I was a fool not to have realized.

"Someone named Ann Shard?" I asked.

"Yes, exactly like that. You must remain—" He stopped talking as he saw my look of consternation. "You've met her?"

"Yesterday. She wanted us to find a gold ring. She had some story about her client's mother or something. We found the ring, but I didn't give it to her because it didn't want to be found and was sticky with negative emotional energy. I didn't want anyone to get hurt."

He frowned and paced some more. "I don't get it. A ring? No ring ever had any power, least of all a curse. It's just one of those dumb stories that get around, like pointy hats and wands and broomsticks and stuff. Hang on a minute. Yes, I've got it. If Shandar was going to get rid of me, then he must have been worried about—"

He didn't get to finish his sentence. Zambini's six minutes were up. He had melted into nonexistence until the next time—if there was a next time.

I sniffed the air and noticed smoke coming up

through the hatch from the C deck. The trolls must have been trying to smoke me out. I ran up the stairs that led to the command deck at the top of the landship and pulled the lever to blow the emergency roof access hatch. The door vanished with an explosive concussion, and I climbed out onto the riveted top of the landship. The trolls were nowhere in sight, so I took the flare pistol from my bag, aimed carefully, and pulled the trigger. There was a sharp crack, and in an instant the marker flare burst high above my head.

"Ha, smoked you out!" came a rumbling voice from behind me, and I found myself staring into the small green eyes of a troll who had climbed up the outside of the landship. I picked up a heavy branch and swung it as hard as I could at his head. It was a futile gesture, of course. The troll smiled cruelly and thrust out a hand to grab me. It would have done so, too, had not the emergency hatch I had blown out not returned to earth at that precise moment and landed on its head. The troll yelled in pain, lost its footing, and fell off the landship.

I looked over the edge.

"What happened?" asked the second troll.

"That one may look small," said the first, rubbing his head tenderly, "but she can sure pack a punch."

"Jenny!"

It was the prince. He had come in for my evacuation

as promised, and I needed no second bidding. I jumped onto the carpet, and we were soon flying back across the Troll Wall to safety.

"That was cutting it a bit close," said Nasil as he expertly held the carpet together on the short journey to the Stirling railroad station. "Did you see him?"

"And how."

TWENTY

Back at Zambini Towers

We took the train back to the Kingdom of Hereford. After the afternoon's action, the carpet was in no state to be used for anything — not even a carpet. The prince had no cash, so he swapped a minor dukedom back in his home Kingdom of Portland for two first-class tickets and we caught the first train out of Stirling station. As a foundling I was not permitted to sit anywhere but third class, but when the conductor questioned my presence in first, the prince said that I was his personal organ donor and traveled everywhere with him, just in case. The conductor congratulated the prince on such a novel use of a foundling and told me I was lucky to have such a kind benefactor.

We made Hereford by ten thirty that night and walked to Kazam by a back route to avoid being seen. Tiger and Perkins were waiting at a window on the ground floor next to the trash cans to let us in, as the Infinite Thinness spell was still very much in force. We dropped into the Palm Court, where Mawgon and Monty Vanguard were just as I had seen them last—stone.

"No change here, then."

"None at all," Tiger said.

"Moobin and the others?"

"Still in jail," replied Perkins as we went back out into the lobby. "I tried to contact Judge Bunty Patel to overturn the king's illegal edict and got as far as the judge's secretary's secretary's secretary. She laughed and asked if I was insane, then hung up. How did it go up north?"

We sat on the sofa in the Kazam offices next to the sleeping form of Kevin Zipp, and I related pretty much everything that Zambini had told me—from the so-called Ann Shard being the Mighty Shandar's agent, to the worthlessness of rings as a conduit of power, to Blix being one of the few people able to work in RUNIX, to Once Magnificent Boo's disfigurement.

"Ouch," said Perkins, looking at his own fingers.

I then told them that Zambini thought magic might have intelligence and would "find a way" to let us win if it had a mind to.

"That's like saying electricity has free will," said Perkins, "or gravity."

"Gravy has free will?" said Tiger. "That explains a lot. I *knew* it didn't like me."

"Not gravy, *gravity.*"

"I'm not sure I buy that."

"Me neither," I replied, "but he's the Great Zambini, so we can't reject the idea totally. He wasn't out of ideas about his own predicament, either. Here."

I handed Perkins the old envelope covered with Zambini's handwritten notes. "He thinks these observations may help us crack the spell that keeps him from returning to us."

"And he said the Mighty Shandar cast it?"

I nodded.

"Not good," Perkins said after studying the notes for a while. "It seems Zambini is locked into a spell with a passthought on auto-evolve; it changes randomly every two minutes. One moment it's all about swans on a lake at sunset, the next, spoonbills in the Orinoco delta. And the very act of entering the passthought changes the passthought. We can't crack Mawgon's code and it's static, so what hope do we have with one that changes?"

We were all silent for a while.

"Did you see any trolls?" asked Tiger.

"Two of them. They think we're vermin."

"We don't like them much, either."

"No, no, they *really* think we're vermin—a pest that needs eradicating. They're entirely indifferent to humans. We're to them as rabbits are to us—only more destructive and less cuddly."

"Oh," said Tiger, who as a Troll War orphan had an interest in trolls. "Then the invasions are even *more* of a waste of life, cash, time, and resources than we had suspected?"

"It looks that way." I took a deep breath and looked at my watch. It was quarter past eleven. Blix's conceding offer ran out at midnight. "Did you talk to the residents about taking Blix's deal?"

Perkins reached into his top pocket and pulled out a notebook. "They may be a bit odd but are quite forthright in their views." He consulted his notes. "I could only speak to twenty-eight of them. Monty Vanguard is stone, Mysterious X and the Funny Smell in room 632 are nebulous at best, the Thing in 346 made a nasty noise when I knocked on the door, and the Lizard Wizard just stared at me and ate insects."

"He does that," I said.

"I'm not totally convinced the Thing in room 346 is a sorcerer at all," remarked Tiger, "nor the Funny Smell."

"Who's going to go and find out? You?"

"On second thought," mused Tiger, "let's just assume they are."

"So anyway," continued Perkins, "the residents have

without exception poured scorn on Blix's offer and announced they would sooner descend into confused old age and die in their beds while subsisting on a diet of rotten cabbage, weak custard, and drippings."

"Isn't that what they're doing already?" asked Tiger.

"Which shows their commitment to things continuing as they are," I said.

"Right," agreed Perkins, "but nearly all of them said they would also trust the judgment of Kazam's manager."

"That's not good," I said. "Mr. Zambini is still missing."

"They didn't mean Zambini," said Perkins, "and even though half of them don't know your name and refer to you as 'the sensible-looking girl with the ponytail,' they're all behind you."

There was more than two thousand years of combined magical experience in the building, and that wealth of knowledge had approved of what I did. All of a sudden, I felt stronger and more confident. But it didn't help with our immediate problems.

"What about you?" I said to Perkins. "Are you going to take the two million moolah?"

Perkins looked at me with a frown. "And miss all this craziness? Not for anything. I'm astonished you even had to ask."

"Thank you."

We said nothing for several moments.

"We found out where the Infinite Thinness enchantment was coming from," said Tiger, "though not who might have cast it."

He went to my desk and waved a pocket shandarmeter above the small terra cotta pot. The needle on the gauge showed a peak reading of two thousand shandars. We didn't know how the enchantment that protected the old building worked, but this was the source.

I joined Tiger and picked the ring out of the pot. It was large, utterly plain, and unremarkable. I had a thought and picked up the phone.

"Are you calling Blix?" asked Perkins.

"No—the Mighty Shandar's agent. We need to find out more."

I dialed the number the so-called Ann Shard had given me, and after two rings someone picked up.

"Miss D'Argento?" I said. "It's Jennifer Strange."

"I can see my impertinent yet wholly necessary subterfuge took a modicum of cerebral activity to divine," she announced in her odd Longspeak, "but in this pursuit you were proved correct."

"Pardon?"

"It took you an entire day to figure out I wasn't Ann Shard."

"Oh," I said. "Yes."

There was a pause before she continued. "Is this communication to impart knowledge about the geographical whereabouts of my client's mother's ring?"

"We haven't got it, if that's what you mean, but yes, it is about the ring. What's so special about it, and why did the Mighty Shandar want it found?"

"There is nothing special about it," she said simply. "You have my word on that."

"And Shandar's reason for wanting it found?"

"We have many clients," said Miss D'Argento in a mildly annoyed tone, "and we never betray their confidence."

Zambini was right; Shandar was behind this. If there wasn't at least some truth in it, she would have simply laughed or dismissed the idea out of hand.

"Is there anything else? Miss D'Argento is really most frightfully busy." She was talking about herself again.

"Yes," I said. "The next time Shandar wakes from granite, tell him that we'll be after him once Zambini is freed — and he will be, mark my words."

"Goodbye, Miss Strange. We'll meet again, I'm sure."

And the phone went dead. I told the others what she had said, but none of it seemed to help much, except perhaps to confirm what we suspected — that the Mighty Shandar was keeping a watchful eye on events here in the

Kingdom of Snodd, and that if Shandar was behind the Great Zambini's disappearance, then it was going to be extra tough getting Zambini back.

"Hullo, Jennifer," said a voice from the sofa. "Did my vision work out?"

"It did; thank you, Kevin."

Kevin Zipp looked tired and drawn. He usually did when he'd been trying extra hard to see into the foggy murk of the yet-to-be.

"Do I get a ten?"

"On both counts."

Tiger dutifully fetched the Visions Book so I could rate Kevin's powers. I turned to the correct page and noted that his last vision, the one by which we had found Zambini, was coded RAD105. I gave him a ten for this, countersigned it, and then gave him ten for RAD095. It took his Correct Vision Strike Average up to seventy-six percent — just out of Remarkable and into Exceptional, but not yet beyond the ninety percent mark and the highest pre-cog accolade of all: Blistering.

"Jenny?" said Tiger, who had been staring at the entries in the Visions Book. "What does that look like to you?"

"RAD105?"

"No, I mean what if the five was an *s*? What would you think then?"

"RADIOS?"

I stared at Tiger and he stared back. The kid was a genius.

"Kevin," I said excitedly, "are you still getting the Vision Boss prediction?"

"I had it again just now. Why?"

"It could mean 'vision BO55.' You may have just had a vision . . . about someone else's past vision."

"That's a first," said Kevin, unfazed by it all, as usual.

Tiger dashed off to the library to fetch the relevant volume of the *Pre-cognitives Gazetteer of Visions.*

"It must have been seen sometime in the mid-seventies to be numbered so low," observed Perkins.

"We'll soon find out."

Tiger returned with a dusty volume and laid it in front of me. I soon found the entry.

"Vision BO55, October 10, 1974," I read, "was seen by Sister Yolanda of Kilpeck."

"Yolanda?" said Tiger. "Cool. What was it about?"

"Doesn't say. It was a private consultation—contents undisclosed."

"If it was Sister Yolanda, it probably will or did come true," said Kevin. "She didn't have many visions, but her strike rate was always good. Who was the recipient?"

I read the name and suddenly felt cold all over.

"Mr. Conrad Blix of Blix Grange, Blix Street, Hereford."

We all looked at one another. Blix was involved in a

strong prophecy from Sister Yolanda, and Kevin had been hinting at it all week, just without knowing it. We'd be fools not to pick up on a lead like this.

"I think we need to know more about that vision — and quickly," said Tiger.

"Easier said than done," I replied. "It was a private consultation. Only Blix would have the details."

"We need someone at iMagic," observed Tiger. "Someone on the inside."

"Who?" asked Perkins. "Corby, Muttney, and Samantha are all loyal to a fault."

I thought for a moment.

"Perkins," I said, "you've just betrayed us."

"I have?"

"Like the worst kind of leaving-the-sinking-ship rat. I want you to accept Blix's offer for two million moolah, get into Blix Grange, go to where Blix keeps his records, and find out what vision BO55 relates to."

"How am I going to do that?"

"I don't know. Guile and ingenuity?"

But Perkins was reluctant. "Blix would never believe me. He'll think it's a trick of some sort."

"You're right," I said. "He'll need convincing."

Reader, I punched him. Right in the eye, a real corker — a punch like I'd never punched anyone, except that time back at the orphanage when Tamara Glickstein was bullying the smaller kids.

"YOW!" yelled Perkins. "What was that for?"

"He'll believe you now. Tell him I went ballistic when you betrayed us. Tell him I've gone a bit crazy."

"No need to lie, then," remarked Perkins grumpily, his eye already beginning to turn purple.

"Better get going," I said, glancing at the clock and then giving him my warmest hug. I even kissed him on the cheek as an apology for the punch. Tiger offered to hug and kiss him, too, but Perkins said, "No, thanks," and went off to make the phone call. It was three minutes to midnight, and Perkins was gone by five after.

Gone, too, with midnight was Kazam's chance to cut a deal with Blix. The die was cast. The contest would go ahead.

And as likely as not, we'd lose.

TWENTY-ONE

Before the Contest

I lay in bed staring at the water-stained ceiling of my room on the second floor of Zambini Towers. It faced east, and the sun woke me every morning—except *this* morning, as I hadn't gone to sleep. Magic contests rarely ended happily and through the years had resulted in recrimination and despair, bruised egos and lifelong feuds. There were always winners and losers, but this was surely the first time in wizidrical contest history that one team did not include a single sorcerer of any sort.

"What are you thinking about?" asked Tiger, who occasionally slept on my floor. He was not yet used to sleeping on his own and often missed the cozy dormitory companionship of eighty other foundlings, all coughing, grunting, and crying.

"I was thinking about how everything would be fine."

"Me, too."

"Actually, I wasn't."

"No," said Tiger, "neither was I."

I went downstairs after my bath and wandered into the office. I made myself a cup of tea and sat down, deep in thought.

"You seem sad," came a low voice with a singsong Scandinavian lilt to it. "Is everything okay?"

I turned to find the Transient Moose staring at me. "You can talk?"

"Three languages," replied the moose. "Swedish, English, and a smattering of Persian."

"Why haven't you spoken before?"

The moose gave a toss of his antlers, which I took to be a moosian shrug. "No one here really shares any of my interests, so there's not much to say."

"What are your interests?"

"Snow . . . female moose . . . grazing . . . getting enough sodium and potassium in my diet . . . snow . . . avoiding being run over . . . snow . . . female moose . . . snow."

"You're not likely to be run over in here," I said,

"or find snow or a female moose—and you don't need sodium, since you're a spell."

"As I said," said the moose, "not much to talk about. Did you like my Infinite Thinness enchantment?"

"That was you?" I asked, with some surprise.

"I didn't like the way they kept on taking the sorcerers away," he said simply, "so I used that thing that didn't want to be found to increase my power."

He nodded toward where the terra cotta pot and ring were located in my desk drawer, and I picked them up and stared at them. It still didn't make any sense.

"How is this working?"

"I have no idea," replied the moose. "It's suffused with emotional power. Loss, hatred, betrayal—you name it. I can almost hear the screams."

"Negative emotional energy? A curse?"

The moose gave another toss of his antlers. "Sort of. But good or bad, I can tap into it and draw as much power as I want. It's like having a sorcerer, sitting right there in that pot."

I had an idea. It was a long shot, admittedly. "What are you like at building bridges?"

"Well," said the moose after some reflection, "we weren't talking to the Siberian elk for a while after the whole cash-for-wolves scandal, and I was instrumental in bringing them to the negotiating table. I was alive then, of course, and real."

"I didn't mean building bridges as in 'making people talk to one another,' I meant building bridges as in actually building bridges."

"Ah," said the moose, "you meant *literally*, rather than *metaphorically*."

I nodded, and the moose gave out a short whinnying noise that might have been a laugh.

"What a suggestion," he said. "A moose, building a bridge?" He paused for a moment, then asked why I wanted him to build a bridge. So I told him all about the contest, and he said that he *thought* something odd had been going on, but wasn't sure, and I said that he could be sure that something *was,* and asked him if he thought he might be able to help.

"There's a lot of power coming out of that terra cotta pot," said the moose thoughtfully. "Probably enough to build a bridge."

I stood up. Perhaps all was not lost. "You need to come and see the remains of the bridge. The contest starts in half an hour."

"Leave the building?" said the moose in a horrified tone. "Out of the question. I haven't been outside since it first opened as the Majestic Hotel in 1815."

"Have you tried?"

"Yes."

"Are you sure?"

"No. And that's not the point," said the moose in the

manner of a moose who had realized it was very much the point. "I'm not leaving the hotel, and that's final."

"Agoraphobic?"

"No, thanks; I've already eaten."

"I heard," I began slowly, "that there is some snow outside — and a female moose. Not to mention some sodium. And most of the town center is pedestrianized, so you won't have to worry about being run over by a car."

"I'm only a spell," said the moose wistfully. "I only *think* those things are important. It's the Mandrake Sentience Protocols; I know I'm not real, but I think I am. In any event, I'm not going outside."

"Final?"

"Final."

And he vanished.

I sighed. It had been worth a try, but we were back to square one again. No sorcerers to do the contest. Not one.

"So let's talk about something else," continued the moose, reappearing as suddenly as he had left. "Are you going to go on a date with the young wizard with the tufty hair?"

"How do you know about me and Perkins?"

"It's all they talk about," he said, presumably referring to the retired ex-sorcerers upstairs. This was news to me, and I wasn't sure I wanted to be the subject of bored sorcerer gossip.

"It's complicated."

"Love always is," said the moose, sighing forlornly. "I'm only a vague facsimile of a moose once alive, but I share some of his emotions: *Ach,* how I miss Liesl and the calves."

"Who are you talking to?" asked Tiger, who had just appeared at the door.

"The moose." I pointed at the moose, who simply stared at me, then at Tiger. "You were saying?" I said to the moose, but he just looked at me blankly and then slowly faded from view.

"Are you okay?" Tiger asked.

"I've been better. Come on, let's go and show some dignity before we get trashed. How do I look?"

I had put on my best dress for the contest, and Tiger was wearing a necktie and had combed his hair. We would at least save face and make an appearance at the start.

We stepped out of Zambini Towers after making quite sure that Margaret "the Fib" O'Leary was looking after the front door and would let us back in. Margaret was one of our "hardly mad at all" sorcerers, and also one of the least powerful — she could tell the most whopping lies and, by skilled distortion of facts and appearances, make you believe them wholeheartedly. As a party trick she would convince guests that down was up, then laugh as everyone started fretting that they might fall onto the ceiling.

Many people had taken a day off work to come and watch the contest, and the road leading toward the medieval bridge now resembled a fairground. There were barbecues selling roadkill pizzas and camel's ears in a bun, and traders selling such merchandise as hats, King Snodd action figures that threaten to execute you when you pull a string, and T-shirts with unfunny slogans like MY DAD WENT TO A MAGIC CONTEST AND ALL I GOT IN OUR DAMP HOVEL WAS BRONCHITIS. There were tents with traveling knee-replacement surgeons, as well as sideshows where you could gawk at "Timothy the Amazing Two-Headed Boy" and other "Quirks of Nature." There was also a tent where you could pay half a moolah to view parts of a troll pickled in a large jar.

"Do you have a half-moolah coin?" asked Tiger.

"Don't even think about it."

As we moved closer to the bridge, we could already see the flag-wavers, jugglers, tumblers, and ventriloquists entertaining the crowds before the warm-up act. We overheard in passing that the halftime bear-debating event was canceled, as the bear had arrived all mellow and wasn't up for an argument.

"They've got a replacement for halftime," said

someone close by. "Jimmy Nuttjob will set himself on fire and then be blasted high above the rooftops from an air cannon while yelling 'God save the king.'"

"Probably hoping for a knighthood," said his friend.

"Definitely—but there must be easier ways to do it," replied the first man.

Tiger and I worked our way to the front, where barriers had been erected to keep the crowds safe from any passive spelling, and showed our IDs to the police on duty. We were permitted to pass, and moved toward a small gaggle of people standing at the edge of the bridge's north abutment, close to the royal observation box. I had no idea what we would do next.

"Ah!" said Blix. "The defenders approach."

He was standing with the rest of iMagic's staff: a weaselly character in ill-fitting clothes named Tchango Muttney, the well-dressed Dame Corby, who wore far more jewelry than was good for her, and Samantha Flynt, who was fantastically pretty but not that bright. I knew this because she had put her pretty floral dress on backwards. Perkins was not with them, but Colonel Bloch-Draine was, and he nodded a gruff greeting in my direction.

"No sorcerers?" asked Blix sarcastically.

"Won't be much of a contest, will it?" I said.

"On the contrary," replied Lord Tenbury, hovering

close at hand. "The best contest requires only a winner—not necessarily any competition."

"And how do you think the crowd will react when they find that the contest has no opposition?"

"The people will not riot," said Tenbury confidently. "After all, a one-sided contest should be cozily familiar to any resident who has ever voted in a Kingdom of Snodd election."

We stopped talking because a colorful parade was approaching, with a shiny brass band, several horsemen, and a retinue of hangers-on; the royal family was arriving in a gilded open-top carriage. Everyone, including me, knelt before our monarch as the carriage stopped and a handy duke offered himself as a step. The king and queen were accompanied by the Spoiled Royal Children: His Royal Petulantness the Crown Prince Steve, who was twelve, and Her Royal Odiousness Princess Shazza, who was fifteen. As their accolades suggested, they spent much of their time stamping their feet and wanting things. No governess ever lasted longer than twenty-six and three-quarters minutes.

A deafening alarum sounded from thirty buglers all dressed traditionally as badgers, and the royal family walked slowly up to where we stood, waving at the citizenry while their footmen tossed coin vouchers into the crowd. They used to throw coins until the king discovered that his ungrateful subjects were spending the cash in non-Snodd-owned shops. The "alms vouchers" are redeemable only at Snoddco's, the well-known and wholly substandard superstore.

"Ah!" said the king. "Lord Tenbury and Court Mystician. Good to see you both. I trust we are to see some sport this morning, hmm? Brave of you to turn up, Miss Strange."

Since we had been spoken to, protocol dictated we could now stand. I couldn't help noticing that Queen Mimosa was looking around for something. I took a deep breath.

"I would be failing in my duty," I said nervously, "if I did not lodge a formal complaint over the fairness of this contest."

"Your displeasure is noted, Miss Strange," said the king. "We will glance at your complaint sometime next year. Shall we proceed?"

"Not yet," said the queen, staring at me. "Are you Jennifer Strange?"

"A *foundling,* my dear," said the king in an unsubtle aside. "Unsuitable for a queen's conversation."

"Shut up, Frank. Miss Strange, where is the Kazam team?"

There was a deathly hush.

"Let us take our seats, my dear," said the king, "I feel the—"

"Your team, Miss Strange?"

"In prison, Your Majesty," I said, curtseying, "awaiting a hearing on Monday."

"I see." Queen Mimosa glared at the king, who seemed to shrink under her withering look. "Are you meaning to tell me that you have imprisoned the entire Kazam team in order to guarantee a victory?"

"Not at all," said the king. "It was entirely coincidental. They were all brigands and villains and scallywags and lawbreakers. Is that not so, Court Mystician?"

"Up to a point, Your Majesty, yes, I think we are agreed on that," Blix replied.

"One of their number attacked the castle last night," added Lord Tenbury, "and caused considerable damage."

"Poppycock," said Queen Mimosa. "I saw the whole thing. A single unarmed carpet rescued someone from the High North Tower. Any damage was done by your own gunners."

"And they will be roundly punished, along with the sorcerers we have in custody," said the king. "I think I have shown considerable restraint. I could have put them all to death, but instead I showed mercy — like you tell me to, Pumpkin."

"The charges are quite serious, my queen," said Tenbury, but Queen Mimosa raised a finger and he did not continue. The courtiers and hangers-on had taken a step back and were pretending to find something else to do.

Queen Mimosa moved closer to her husband and lowered her voice. "Listen here, you inbred, pompous little twit. I didn't arrange with Mother Zenobia to have the bridge rebuilt in aid of the Troll War Widows Fund to have you hijack it for your own money-grabbing agenda. Release the Kazam sorcerers immediately, or I will make life so unpleasant that you will wish to have been born a foundling."

"We will discuss this later, my dear."

"We are discussing it now." Her look of thunder would have impressed Lady Mawgon. "Do you doubt *for even one second* that I would not do as I say?"

The king took a deep breath and puffed out his cheeks. He looked around at the ten thousand or so subjects eagerly awaiting the contest. It looked to me as though the king knew well that Queen Mimosa could make his life very unpleasant indeed.

"Lord Tenbury," said the king, "I think we owe it to the citizenry of Snodd to put on a good show. They have come to see a magical contest, and they shall. Release the wizards. I command it."

Blix and Tenbury looked shocked and exchanged desperate glances. There was a very good reason they had hobbled Kazam. I tried not to get excited at our momentary change in fortune—we were still a long way from even catching up. In a panic, Lord Tenbury started patting his pockets in an absent-minded way.

"If you are going to claim you've lost the keys to the city jail, Lord Chief Advisor," snarled the king in a low voice while smiling and waving to the crowd, "I will put your head on a spike and have dogs eat your corpse."

"Here they are," said Lord Tenbury, suddenly finding the keys. "I will see to your instructions this moment, my lord. Miss Strange, you shall accompany me when the car arrives."

"Happy now, Pumpkin?" said the king to Queen Mimosa.

"I love it when you do the right thing, Bunny-wunny," she said, tweaking his royal ear affectionately. She took her leave with the now-bickering Spoiled Royal Children while the king hung back for a moment.

"If Kazam wins," I heard him say to Blix and Tenbury in a low voice, "I will have you both stuffed alive with sawdust and use you for bayonet practice. Do you understand?"

He didn't wait for a reply, and turned to me with such a hateful glare that I took an involuntary step backwards. But he made no comment, and strode toward the royal box to join his family, including his Useless Brother, the royal hanger-on cousins, and his odd-looking mother, the Duck-Faced Dowager Duchess of Dinmore.

The king stepped up to the royal microphone and

made a long, rambling speech about how proud he was that the hard toil of a blindly trusting citizenry kept him and his family in the lap of luxury while war widows begged on the streets, and how he thanked providence that he had been blessed to rule over a nation whose inexplicable tolerance toward corrupt despots was second to none. The speech was well received, and some citizens were even moved to tears. Then the king ordered that the contest begin.

"We'll still thrash you," Blix told me, "and if you're worried about your darling boyfriend, he's quite safe for the moment."

My heart fell. Perkins had been rumbled.

"I don't know what you mean."

"No? Here." And he passed me the left-handed conch that we'd given Perkins.

"If any harm comes to him," I said between gritted teeth, "I will hold you personally responsible."

"Oh, oh, I'm so frightened," replied Blix sarcastically. "Now, piss off. Haven't you got some wizards to spring from jail?"

"I'll be back with help," I said, "and you'll be thrashed. And just for the record, he's not my boyfriend."

Blix laughed and had his first two stones fitted even before Lord Tenbury's car arrived to take Tiger and me to fetch the sorcerers.

TWENTY-TWO

Bridge Building

So which two do you want released?" asked Lord Tenbury as we arrived outside the city jail. It was a large stone building north of the city known ironically as the Hereford Hilton, much to the annoyance of the *real* Hereford Hilton coincidentally located two doors down, something that worked to the advantage of the prisoners when pizza deliveries were misdirected.

"I was under the impression His Majesty specifically requested that *all* be released," I pointed out.

"Then you understand little of the role of the lord chief advisor. My duty is to serve my king the best way I can and interpret his orders as I see fit. Two sorcerers. Choose now."

I could see it was the best deal I was going to get, and every second spent arguing was a second wasted. I could apologize to the Price brothers later.

"The Wizard Moobin," I said without hesitation, "and . . . Patrick of Ludlow."

Lord Tenbury relayed the orders to the jailer, told us we could make our way back to the bridge on our own, and was gone. A half hour later Moobin and Patrick emerged, blinking in the daylight. They had their lead finger cuffs removed, and within a few seconds we were in a taxi heading back toward the bridge.

"Well done," said Moobin, brushing the dirt, earwigs, and other prison detritus from his jacket.

"Don't thank me," I said, annoyed with myself that I had done so little. "Thank Queen Mimosa."

"She's an ex-sorcerer herself," he said. "I think she has a soft spot for us. Who else do we have on the team?"

"You two are it."

Team Kazam was going be severely underpowered. I told them what had happened since their imprisonment: Mawgon was still stone, her passthought unbroken; Perkins had been captured in an attempt to uncover a missing vision; Transient Moose had turned out to be semi-self-aware and was the agent behind the Infinite Thinness spell, and Zambini hadn't really been much help—although it had been good to see him.

"The moose was drawing power from a ring?" said

Moobin, incredulous. "From a band of *gold,* the single-most boringly nonreactive metal on the planet?"

"Zambini was surprised it had such power, too."

"Well, it's not important right now," Moobin said as the taxi dropped us as close as possible to the south bridge abutment. "We're going to have to wing it a bit and break a few magic rules. The future of Kazam is in the balance, and we have to work together if we're to have any chance of survival. Now, listen carefully . . ."

As Tiger took the cab back to Zambini Towers to put his part of the plan in motion, Moobin, Patrick, and I surveyed the wreckage of what had once been a stone bridge with five arches supported by four piers. iMagic had already had an hour's start, and the bridge piers on their side had been cleared of old rubble and stood three feet above the water level. The stones were moving about their site steadily, to many "oohs" and "aahs" from the onlookers. It took a moment for us to be noticed by the audience, but then there was a sudden hush followed by a cheer. Blix's history of hasty, substandard wizidrical building work had severely dented his popularity in town. As the cheer echoed around the area, Patrick levitated ten pieces of cut stone from the riverbed simultaneously, then moved them in a long procession to be stacked for later insertion in the bridge.

The crowd went wild at this, and the scoreboard,

offering up-to-the-second live betting odds, moved us up from 1000:1 against to 500:1 against. Not great, but an improvement. I saw Patrick hold on to a crowd barrier for support after his exertions. He would not have attempted such a feat if Moobin hadn't requested it — the purpose was to make the iMagic team nervous. It worked. Two stones about to be placed dropped into the river with a heavy splash as the iMagic team lost concentration.

"Patrick will need continuous food if he does most of the heavy lifting," said Moobin, exercising each of his index fingers in preparation. "Better check to see how Tiger is doing."

I needed no second bidding. I called a street urchin out of the crowd and deputized him onto the Kazam team in order to keep Patrick and Moobin supplied with water and food, and told him to find a seamstress to repair their clothes on the fly, as continuous heavy spelling unravels stitching.

"To battle," said Moobin as he walked across the scaffolding footbridge that ran parallel to the stone bridge. He lifted stones from the rubble with a relaxed movement of his hands, and sorted them into categories of dressed, rubble, and ornate. It was mostly bravado. As with Patrick, it took a lot more power than Moobin made out. If they tried to keep it up like this, they'd be exhausted long before our half of the bridge was finished.

"Surprised to see me, Blix?" said Moobin as they met in the middle of the footbridge.

"It won't make any difference," Blix sneered back. "The iMagic team is on a roll."

It certainly appeared that way. The piers were now nine feet high, and iMagic was making good progress on their first arch.

"We'll see."

They parted to continue their work, while I hurried off to see Tiger.

Zambini Towers is located in the tight network of streets near the cathedral, no more than a three-minute jog from the bridge. By the time I got there, Tiger was already organizing the retired sorcerers, wizards, and enchanters into groups, in order to transfer the wizidrical power from the housebound Transient Moose all the way down to the bridge.

We placed two sorcerers at each street corner, stretching from Zambini Towers to the bridge. One index finger of a sorcerer would pick up the crackle, and the other would send it on to the next, like a daisy chain. With teams of two, the sorcerers could relieve each other when they got tired and have someone to remind them what they were supposed to be doing.

"How's it going?" I asked.

"Almost done," replied Tiger, "but you need to speak to the moose yourself—he just stares blankly at me."

I found the moose gazing at the spreading boughs of the oak tree growing in the lobby.

"Was this here yesterday?" he asked.

"It's been there for almost twenty years," I replied.

"Well, I never. What can I do for you?"

The Thinness enchantment was no longer needed now that the contest had begun, and it didn't take long to convince the moose to channel the power from the small terra cotta pot toward the bridge—or, to be more precise, to Edgar Znorpp at the front entrance, who would then pass it to Deirdre Karamazov waiting on the street outside, who would pass it to the next. This was the Mysterious X, who had enclosed himself in an empty pickle jar as protection against the wind.

"Just say when," replied the moose with a carefree toss of his antlers, "and Moobin and Patrick will be able to draw as much power as I can extract from that pot."

"Will you be all right?" I asked.

"Never better," he replied, "and thanks for asking."

I told Tiger to stand by for my signal, then visited all our retired sorcerers on the way to the bridge. They were set and ready. It would only take a minor lapse in concentration for one to break the chain, and I was hoping desperately that they could put their eccentricities aside for just long enough. Margaret O'Leary was last in line, and chosen specifically because she was the least bonkers and the best liar in case anyone asked what she was up to.

"Don't let it flow to the iMagic team by accident," I said, and she assured me she would not. I signaled to Moobin and Patrick, who were watching me, then spoke to Tiger through the conch to instruct the moose to start channeling.

It happened fast. I saw Margaret stiffen slightly as the power started to flow through her. Her braid unraveled and both earrings fell out of her ears. She didn't even notice.

"Wow," she said with a smile, "that's good crackle. Can I pinch some to deal with a few gray hairs?"

"At the end, if all goes well."

I watched Moobin and Patrick as the power flowed through to them, and the effect was almost instantaneous. Moobin lifted two stones in unison and clicked them into place on the far side of the bridge as easily as if they were Lego. There was a gasp from the crowd, then a resounding cheer; our odds on the scoreboard rose from 500:1 to 50:1 against.

I breathed a small sigh of relief. At least we were now actually in the game, even if far behind. The iMagic team completed their first arch within another five minutes and then moved on to the next.

I spent the next hour moving up and down the daisy

chain to ensure all was well. It was vital that the areas between the sorcerers remained relatively clear and no one lingered too long within the streams — passive spelling was a very real risk, and it sapped power. There was a minor hiccup when a van parked in the way; we had to interrupt the stream while we moved the sorcerers to the other side of the road. But it all worked, and within that hour, Kazam started to catch up. Soon we were only one arch behind iMagic.

"Impressive," said Blix as I hurried past him with some chocolate for Patrick, "but you can't keep up that rate of sustained spelling forever."

"We'll see."

Tiger and I made sure the sorcerers kept cool by drinking gallons — and I mean gallons — of ice water; being a conduit for wizidrical energy without actually using it makes one grow hot, as a wire does when an electrical current passes through. We also had to ensure that the changeovers went smoothly when, predictably enough, a sorcerer needed a visit to the bathroom. And we had to do all this subtly, without alerting Blix to what we were up to.

Within another twenty minutes we were even with iMagic, and half an hour after that, we had passed them. We were now in the lead, reflected by the odds on the scoreboard and much to the delight of the crowd. There was less delight from the king, who sat in the royal box tapping his fingers impatiently on his second-best throne.

Blix paused for a moment and walked over to Moobin and me. He looked at us each in turn, then gave a rare smile. "Where are you getting all this power?"

"Skill, hard work, and efficient use of resources," replied Moobin. "You should try it someday."

"Very funny." Blix thought for a moment, then abruptly changed his manner. "Okay, here it is, with me eating humble pie: Congratulations. You've bested me."

Moobin and I looked at each other.

"A trick of some sort, Blix?" asked Moobin, not pausing for one second as he set a carved piece of stone in place. "We're barely half an arch ahead."

"We're almost worn out," he replied. "Corby and Muttney have been . . . disappointing. Perhaps we can negotiate my defeat so I am not utterly humiliated?"

It was an astonishing request. In answer, Moobin was firm but clear. "We will give you the same courtesy and kindness you gave us, Blix."

"How unpleasant of you," he said after a pause. "What happened to all the 'brother wizard' stuff?"

"It evaporated when you had us all thrown into jail."

"Really?" Blix asked, as though it had only just occurred to him that we might be annoyed. "Yes, I suppose it might. Never mind. I will go and draft a letter conceding my position. But we should finish the bridge, yes? A good show for the king and the citizenry?"

"I agree," said Wizard Moobin suspiciously.

Blix gave us another smile and moved off to speak to the colonel, who had been hovering close by.

"I strongly suggest that we don't relax for a moment," I said as soon as Blix and the colonel had departed in some haste. "I smell a very large Blix-shaped rat up to something."

"I agree," said Moobin. "But what?"

I didn't know, and left the sorcerers to carry on while the iMagic team, now without their leader, began to fall further and further behind. By the time we had our second arch almost finished, the odds on the scoreboard made us the clear favorites and iMagic merely washed-up old has-beens.

But just as Kazam was about to start on our final arch, something happened.

TWENTY-THREE

The Surge

It was a surge—a burst of almost unprecedented violence. Oddly, it went only through Patrick and Moobin; the iMagic sorcerers were unaffected. The heavy blocks that Patrick and Moobin had been moving suddenly flew high into the air. One fell on an overpass two hundred yards away, where we heard the sound of cars braking and colliding, and another plunged into the river. Two others, each a quarter of a ton, were thrown so high that they disappeared from sight.

Moobin swore as he tried to control the surge. He described it later like being in a car with no brakes and the throttle jammed full-on while trying to negotiate the Saint Nigel's Day parade without hitting anyone. To absorb the raw energy entering his body, he pointed his fingers at the river. In an instant the water had changed to a cheap German white wine and receded in both directions, revealing a lot of mud and more shopping carts than I thought even existed.

I looked across at Patrick. He, too, was struggling to do something with the massive surge, and had switched his attention to what he usually did — lift cars for the city's illegal-parking department. All cars within a 250-yard radius were violently lifted three feet into the air; when this wasn't enough to absorb the power, Patrick began moving them all toward the impound lot two miles away.

I bit my lip. An oversurge of this strength was likely to end in one way: when the power overcame the sorcerers completely and caused them to burst. It would be painful and very messy. I watched with growing panic as the increased power started to invade Patrick and Moobin's thoughts and random spells began to bubble up from their subconscious. There was a brief shower of toads, dogs started barking, and everyone in the crowd who had curly hair found that it had straightened. The river turned from cheap wine to an expensive 1928 Château Latour, every watch in the area reset itself to midday, and the clouds above the city formed into barnyard-animal shapes.

Just when I thought our sorcerers could take no

more, the surge stopped. The wine-river washed back, the cloud shapes and toads vanished, and in the distance we could hear Patrick's cars fall with expensive-sounding crunches. Moobin and Patrick dropped to their knees, their index fingers purple with bruises that had spread across their hands and up their forearms. It would be painful for them to spell for weeks.

I ran up to Moobin as the crowd started to murmur excitedly. Blix's team—minus Blix himself, who was nowhere to be seen—was staring at us, open-mouthed. They'd never seen anything like it, either.

"Check the chain," muttered Moobin. "Make sure everyone's okay."

Tiger and I dashed back down the daisy chain to see if anyone had burst. The first link was Margaret O'Leary, who was standing on the corner by a sideshow tent, where the Two-Headed Boy had popped his heads out of the tent flap to witness the event.

"What in Shandar's name was *that?*" she said. "I just channeled more power in thirty seconds that I've expended in a lifetime."

"Has Blix come by here?"

"No."

Next in the chain was Bartleby the Bald, who was in much the same state—in shock, but okay. Tiger and I worked our way back to Zambini Towers and were relieved to find that although the sorcerers were hot and sweaty and bruised with the effort, none had dared break the chain, and for good reason. A sorcerer who had broken the chain would have borne the full brunt of the surge. The only safe option had been to hope that those at the end could safely expel the extra power.

"You check the moose," I said to Tiger. "I'll look in on Lady Mawgon and Monty Vanguard."

I looked into the Palm Court, but Mawgon and Monty were unchanged. Wherever the power was coming from, it wasn't stored in the Dibble coils — they remained as resolutely full and unhacked as before.

"Jenny!" came Tiger's voice. "In here!"

I dashed through to the lobby, where Tiger was kneeling next to a blackened moose-shaped hole burned into the carpet. There were similar burned shapes on each of the four walls, too — neat moosian front, back, and side elevations — and a perfect moose-shaped hole burned through the ceiling for three stories up. It was so precise you could see the delicate splay of the antlers.

"He said it was the only way to stop the surge," said ex-weather-monger Taylor Woodruff IV, who was standing close by. "He had to take the full force internally. He said he was sorry if it messed up your bridge building."

Tiger and I walked in silence to the office, musing over the once Transient's Moose's passing. He had frazzled every single line of the spell that made up his existence and vanished in a brief blast of energy. I stood at my desk and picked up the small pot with the ring in it. The ring's enormous power still didn't make any sense. Not to me, not to anyone—and not to Tiger, who hated unanswered questions more than anyone.

"Look," he said, showing me the readout from the shandargraph. There were multiple peaks due to the surge we had just seen, but also *another* drain, sustained over thirty-seven seconds, and peaking at 1.2 gigashandars. The range and direction were the same as Kazam's surge: up around the old bridge somewhere.

"Was that Blix?" asked Tiger.

"If it was, he didn't use it on the bridge," I said, looking at my watch. It had been reset to midday in the surge, and now read eight minutes past.

"One-point-two gigashandars?" queried Tiger. "Isn't that the power-drain requirement of a—"

"It is. Call 999 and mutter 'Quarkbeast' in a panicky voice. I need Once Magnificent Boo at the bridge as soon as possible."

"You think—?"

"I do. The Quarkbeast that was on the loose has just divided."

TWENTY-FOUR

Risk of Confluence

I ran back to the bridge to find Moobin and Patrick sucking on ice cubes and trying to get their breath back. The iMagic team was still working, but without Blix they were a good four hours behind, if they could finish at all.

"The moose is gone," I said to Moobin, "so you're on your own. The surge you felt was a power drain as something latched onto the ambient wizidrical energy and drew what it needed through you. It was Blix's Plan B, a plan he hatched with the help of the colonel. This is no longer a magic contest — it's an assassination attempt!"

"To what end?"

"To put Blix on the throne. With the Court Mystician eighth in line, everyone who stands between Blix and the crown is here today, gathered conveniently in one place to suffer—death by Quarkbeast!"

"A bit of a long shot," replied Moobin doubtfully. "The last person savaged by a Quarkbeast was attacked over a decade ago, and he did provoke it with a garden fork. I can't see the king attacking anything with a garden fork."

"He'd have a footman do it for him," said Margaret O'Leary, who had joined us, "but I'm not sure a Quarkbeast would be able to make the distinction between the attacker and person who ordered it."

"Not that way," I replied, still out of breath from the run. "I mean with a Confluence. Place a captured Quarkbeast next to a source of heavy spelling, and it will draw the vast quantity of power needed to divide itself. It tried earlier with Patrick when he was moving the oak for the colonel, but it couldn't draw enough. The moose gave it as much as it needed—and more."

"But if the two new beasts are not separated after division," said Moobin, who knew a bit about Quarkbeasts, too, "then—"

"Right," I said. "If the two beasts aren't separated within a thousand seconds, the Quarkbeast will recombine with enough energy to take out a third of the city."

They stared at me, horrified.

"How long is a thousand seconds?" Margaret O'Leary asked.

"Sixteen minutes and forty seconds." I looked at my watch. It was eleven minutes past. If the Quarkbeast had divided when the surge ended, we had less than five minutes left. We looked around. Most of the south of the city would be taken out and with it, King Snodd and all his family, half the police, most of the Imperial Guard, all the spectators — and us. Blix would be taking cover somewhere out of the blast radius.

"No witnesses," said Moobin, "and no one to refute whatever version of events King Blix decided. He could blame the explosion on anything he chose."

"We need to find a locked room within fifty meters of the royal box," I muttered. "Wait here."

I ran across to where Lord Tenbury was standing, presumably wondering whether the king was serious about stuffing him and Blix with sawdust if they lost the contest. I explained as briefly as I could what was up. Tenbury, eager to regain the king's trust and knowing full well that Blix could never be trusted, immediately ordered the royal family's evacuation, then returned to us to see how he could help. He might have been corrupt, but he was no coward.

"Where do we start?" asked Moobin. "There must be hundreds of rooms big enough to hide two mirror-image Quarkbeasts."

Word was getting out that something was up—the hurried way in which the royal family was removed, most likely, and then the Imperial Guard itself, which had a reputation for running from danger. The crowd began to grow restless, and when those in the expensive seats started to move away, their jewelry rattling in a panicked fashion, those in the cheaper seats also decided to make a run for it.

As I looked around to see where a Quarkbeast might be hidden, a notion came into my head. "Moobin! Perkins is imprisoned with the Quarkbeast!"

"You *know* this or you *think* this? We don't have time to make a mistake."

I had to make a swift judgment call. Half of Hereford and thousands of lives depended upon it.

"I *know* this," I said, taking a deep breath, "because it's an odd notion that popped uninvited into my head. And if Perkins has any particular skill, it's that of seeding ideas. I think he might be trying to communicate with me."

I closed my eyes and tried to empty my mind, which was difficult in the noise of the mass exit of spectators.

"Moobin," I said, "I need you to take out all my senses."

He pointed his bruised finger at me, and after a false start, everything went empty. It was as though I had fallen into an empty space within me where there was nothing but time, thoughts, smells, and the deep red of the sky at dawn. It was extraordinarily peaceful, and without the distraction of overwhelming sensory input, I felt unusually clear-headed. At first I could sense nothing except the jumble of my own thoughts and the smell of bacon and Irish stew, but after a moment or two I forced these to one side. All of a sudden, there was a small voice on the very edge of my conscious mind, where the froth of random thoughts meets free will.

It was Perkins, and he was sending me ideas. But he wasn't that good at it, so the message came across like a telegram, and what's more, one that was badly spelled.

. . . WEST OF SNOOD BLVD SELLAR ++ KWARKBEAST DIVIDED ++ EXPLOD EMMENINT ++ THREE STEPS DOUN ++ STILL WANT DATE? ++ REPEAT SNOOD BLVD SELLAR ++ KWARK-BEAST . . .

And so it repeated. I listened to it three times, each time spelled differently, until Moobin brought me back to the world of heat, light, and sound.

Once Magnificent Boo and Tiger were just arriving in the Quarkbeast containment vehicle. I told everyone what I'd heard as my watch marked thirteen minutes since the surge. Three minutes to go.

"Anyone who wants to head for safety has to leave now," I said. "No one will think any worse of you for it."

No one made a move. Not even Lord Tenbury.

"Right," I said. "Follow me."

Snodd Boulevard ran from the cathedral to the north end of the bridge. After a hurried search we found a house with three steps down to a locked green-painted cellar door. Patrick pulled it off its hinges with a powerful flourish of his bruised hands, and we hurried in to find ourselves in a long corridor with doors on either side, all locked.

"Where now?" asked Tiger as our final minute began to tick away.

"Doorknobs," growled Boo. "Find the warm one."

Moobin found it, and once Patrick had again torn the door from its hinges we found a small storage room with a vaulted ceiling and a single window high in the end wall. Perkins was lying cuffed, bound, and gagged near the doorway.

And at the far end of the chamber were two equal but opposite Quarkbeasts.

One of them was the one I had seen around town earlier, but the other was mine—the one I had lost up on the Dragonlands. Every detail was the same: the sixth thoracic scale slightly askew, the right front dew claw missing, and even the single white foot. I wasn't quite sure how, but my Quarkbeast was back.

I took all this in on that first glance, and also noted a high-pitched hum in the air. But another fact trumped all others: They were almost touching. Our thousand seconds were nearly up.

"Still!" said Boo, and we all froze. The low hum rose in pitch as the Quarkbeasts moved closer to each other. It reached a whine, then lowered again as they moved a few inches apart. This was the Song of the Quarkbeast.

Others who have heard it are now little more than dust. But if I was about to die, then I was glad to have heard the song. It was lonely — one of lament, of unknown knowledge. A song of resignation, of poetry given and received. The small movements that the Quarkbeasts made as they padded around each other altered the hum so subtly that it sounded like an alto bassoon, but with one single note, infinitely variable.

But it wasn't a song of peace, love, or happiness. It was a requiem — for all of us. We stood stock-still. No one dared move in case the Quarks became startled and recombined through fear, mischief, or boredom.

But I had to do something. I said the first thing that came into my head.

"Hello, boy."

The new Quarkbeast turned to look at me, and its

mauve eyes flashed a sense of recognition. It looked at its partner, then at me again.

"I still have much to do," I said softly. "Adventures. *Wonderful* adventures. And I'm not sure I can do them without you."

It wagged its tail as if it understood, but it remained where it was. The low hum rose in pitch as the other Quarkbeast paced around it.

"Walkies," said Tiger from out in the corridor. The Quarkbeast recognized his voice, too, and apparently eager to drag Tiger around the neighborhood once again, it gave one final look at its partner and padded out to where Tiger was waiting.

The low hum stopped, and Once Magnificent Boo moved cautiously forward with some aluminum-coated zinc treats to tempt the other Quarkbeast.

"Welcome back," I said.

"Quark," said the Quarkbeast.

Within a few short moments, Boo had steered the original Quarkbeast out of the room and into the riveted titanium crate, then driven it back to the railroad station, where she dispatched it off to Australia. The danger was over.

I untied Perkins, who gave me an awkward hug and thanked me for tuning in to his thoughts.

"Hey," I said with a smile. "What girl doesn't like

being thought about?" I had a sudden realization. "By the way, did I detect you thinking about asking me out for a date while you were directing us to you?"

"I couldn't help it," said Perkins, looking somewhat embarrassed. "Maybe the idea of sharing a Potage Jojolie at the dreary-chic Dungeon Rooms helped me to forget that I was about to be annihilated."

"In that case," I said, "I guess you better book us a table."

We walked out into the daylight and back the short distance to the north abutment, where the unfinished bridge lay before us. The iMagic team had fled the scene, Lord Tenbury had marched off with a determined air, and of the crowds, only the fearless, stupid, and sleeping remained. The scoreboard still displayed the final odds — 100:1 in favor of Kazam.

We jumped when an explosive report came from behind us and a flaming figure shot high into the air. It was Jimmy "Daredevil" Nuttjob, performing his halftime act. He arced high above our heads, trailing smoke as he went, but disappointingly only managed to get as far as "God save the . . ." before he landed with a splash and a hiss in the river. We clapped dutifully as he surfaced, coughing and spluttering.

"Quark," said the Quarkbeast approvingly.

We sat gathering our thoughts until the lord chief advisor strode up ten minutes later.

"Recent events have changed His Majesty's mood," Tenbury said. "Ex–Court Mystician Blix is wanted for high treason, along with his accomplice Colonel Bloch-Draine, and I am directed to proclaim in His Majesty's name that you are the winners of the contest. Never mind that the bridge is not yet fully built."

We looked at one another. We were all tired and bruised. Somehow jumping around and punching the air seemed inappropriate, given that we had been just ten seconds from dark eternity.

"What about the others?" said Moobin.

Lord Tenbury took a deep breath. "In addition, I will have the Price brothers released immediately, and all charges are to be dropped. I will be making a full and truthful account of your exploits to His Majesty forthwith, and will recommend that the position of Court Mystician be transferred from Mr. Blix to a sorcerer of Kazam's choosing. In addition, I have known His Majesty a long time, and I foresee medals. Lots of them. Probably big and very shiny."

"I have a better idea," said the Wizard Moobin. "No sorcerer at Kazam will want the job of Court Mystician, and we certainly don't want medals. We want to be left alone to pursue the Great Zambini's stated goal to use magic for the good of mankind. We don't want special favors; we simply want justice."

"I'll see that you get it."

"Do that. And remember: We don't respond well to being double-crossed."

"We also require immunity," I said, always thinking of my paperwork, "from prosecution for all spells undertaken today, by anyone."

Lord Tenbury was in no position to do deals. We could have asked for a pink elephant each—and gotten it.

"Leave it with me," he said, and bowed low before departing.

We stood there for a moment, wondering what to do next. Blix could be anywhere by now, and although a nationwide arrest warrant could bring him back to Snodd to stand trial, he wouldn't allow himself to be found. For a sorcerer of Blix's power, staying hidden would be easy.

"How about some lunch?" I announced in a cheery voice as soon as Once Magnificent Boo had joined us after her trip to the train station.

Boo grumbled, but after I pointed out that she was one Quarkbeast closer to enlightenment thanks to us, she shrugged and agreed to come along—as long as we didn't mention the *m*-word in her company.

TWENTY-FIVE

Lunch at Last

We could sense the air of excitement long before we walked into the dining room at Zambini Towers. We were met with a roar of applause and a standing ovation for Patrick and Moobin. By directing the excess energy efficiently, they had done very little damage, and none of it permanent.

The surge had not left the retired sorcerers entirely unharmed. Most had severe bruising to their fingers and an outbreak of warts, but six had also suffered passive spelling. The mildest was simply a case of migrated ear, while the worst was Francesca Derwent, who spent the next two weeks as a codfish. She recovered fully, aside from a tendency to gape a little too much, and her eyes were just a teensy-weensy bit too close to the sides of her head for comfort.

For all the retired sorcerers, it was the first piece of truly practical magic they had committed outside the hotel walls for several decades. Almost all recognized Once Magnificent Boo, and although she began sulky and reticent, she soon moved from utter silence to monosyllables. I knew I could never persuade her to move to Zambini Towers, but her magicozoology expertise would be invaluable in the future.

The Price brothers turned up in time for dessert, straight out of prison and eager to know how it had all turned out. They were immediately set upon by Boo, who demanded to know if any Quarkbeasts had been harmed in their Cambrian thermowizidrical detonation tests in the eighties; the Prices, while unwilling to explain their methodology for obvious reasons, were happy to confirm that no Quarkbeasts had been hurt.

"Okay," said Boo.

"Quark," said the Quarkbeast in a relieved tone.

After that was settled, the Wizard Moobin made a speech and said several things about my conduct that made me blush and stare at the silverware. Tiger and Perkins were mentioned, we had a moment of silence for the no-longer Transient Moose, and we welcomed the Quarkbeast back into the fold.

And that was when Samantha Flynt of iMagic

appeared at the door of the dining room. There was a sudden hush as everyone stared at her. She looked as though she had been crying, and was every bit as annoyingly pretty and perfect close up as she was from a distance.

"Are you staring because she's so lovely?" I said to Perkins.

"Not at all," he replied unconvincingly. "It's because I didn't expect to see her here."

She was invited in and offered some food, which after we explained was always this bad, she accepted gratefully.

"I'm sorry," she sniffed, "but I didn't know where to go."

"There, there," said Moobin, offering her his handkerchief.

She explained that Blix had helped snare the stray Australian Quarkbeast, but she didn't know the details of Blix's attempt to seize power, nor where he was now. The colonel, apparently, would have been made lord chief advisor had Blix's plot to ascend the throne succeeded.

"Can I stay?" she said, dabbing her eyes.

"Absolutely, my dear," said Moobin.

"Samantha Flynt is very pretty, isn't she?" said Kevin Zipp dreamily once she had left the table to go to the restroom.

"I thought that a bit, at *first*," replied Perkins, glancing at me, "but not anymore."

We listened for a moment as Moobin tried to answer a question about suddenly being on the receiving end of more crackle than was safe to handle. "I was lucky to have Patrick with me," he said. "If I'd had to offload all that power on my own, I wouldn't be here now."

We all nodded sagely, and I turned back to Perkins. "Close call, wasn't it?"

"It was worth it to hear the Song of the Quarkbeast."

"Quark," said the Quarkbeast, who was under the table chewing on a saucepan.

"I don't think we should hear it again," I mused. "Twice would be pushing our luck. Listen, I'm sorry for sending you to Blix. I didn't know he'd see through you so easily."

"That was my fault," Perkins said cheerily. "It was all going well until he found me going through his filing cabinet. I should have locked the door. I'm new to all this cloak-and-dagger stuff. He realized I hadn't really defected, and in a twinkling he reduced all his records to rice pudding."

This was disappointing. "I guess we'll never know about Vision BO55, then."

"Oh, I found that out," said Perkins. "Blix caught me *after* I read it."

Tiger and I stared at him. Even the Quarkbeast looked interested.

"The vision was nothing specific," said Perkins. "It

just stated that Blix's wife would be greater and more powerful than he, and ultimately the agent of his downfall."

"He's not married," said Full Price. "Sorcerers rarely are. So what does it relate to?"

We all looked at Kevin Zipp for an answer. "Search me," he said. "It wasn't my vision, anyway—it was Sister Yolanda's. But if she says he's married, then I suppose he will be—or was, or is."

We mused about this for a moment. Sister Yolanda was usually right, but without Blix here to question, it would have to remain a mystery.

"Look," I said. "Dame Corby."

She was standing at the door as self-consciously as a latecomer to her own party. With her was Tchango Muttney, and behind them both, Samantha.

"She doesn't *look* as though the ants obey her," said Tiger. Dame Corby was a rather small, ineffective-looking woman who didn't like to look anyone in the eye.

"iMagic is finished; the traitor Blix has fled," announced Dame Corby in a resigned voice. "We humbly beg to join your establishment in whatever capacity you think fit." She looked at Tchango, who nodded, looking utterly humiliated.

It was embarrassing for us, too, to hear a licensed sorcerer beg in this manner. It also proved what we had thought for some time: Dame Corby's shares in the family trouser-press business were not doing as well as she had boasted.

"You are welcome here," said Moobin as he strode forward to greet them in the traditional way, "but your status and duties will be decided by a committee led by our acting manager."

Moobin introduced them, and they shook my hand in a doubtful manner. I knew for a fact that Blix had referred to me as "that upstart foundling," and it looked as if they shared the sentiment.

"I have heard great things about you," said Dame Corby in a voice taut with forced politeness.

"I, too," said Tchango.

"I'm Samantha Flynt," said Samantha in a breezy tone, giving me her hand to shake, "but it's pronounced without the first *a*."

"Smantha?"

"That's it. I don't have my license yet, but I'm working very hard on my studies. It's tricky because, well," — she tapped her temple with a fingertip — "I don't have much upstairs. Why are you staring at me?"

I took a step back and nudged Moobin.

"What?" he said.

"Shifter," I said out of the corner of my mouth.

"You're going to have to speak up. I can't hear you."

"SHAPE-SHIFTER!" I said, and pointed unsubtly at the apparently pretty girl in front of me. Then Moobin understood, and had a standard Magnaflux Reversal on her in a heartbeat in order to uncover Blix hiding within.

Surprisingly, there was no effect at all except that her ringlets disappeared, her nose became slightly less cute, her eyes reduced in size and blueness, and her waist size increased. A Magnaflux Reversal reversed *all* spells, irrespective of who cast them. Samantha had been augmenting herself.

"Whoops," she said, putting a hand to her nose. "This is like, *so* embarrassing." But we had more important things to worry about than Samantha's vanity.

"Samantha, were you here ten minutes ago?" I demanded.

"It's without the first *a*."

"*Smantha,* were you here earlier?"

Her now not-so-large eyes opened wide. "Absolutely not!"

Samantha had remained Samantha for the simple reason that she *was* Samantha. The first one had been the impostor. There was only one person it could be — and he hadn't returned from the bathroom.

"Blix is in the building!" I yelled. "Containment Plan D!"

We had several plans ready in case of emergency. Plan D was for something nasty that can't be allowed to get out of the hotel. A few weeks back we'd used it on a phantasm that managed to escape from its bell jar, and it was quite a job to get it back in — especially risky because Plan D seals the building, and there is only about four days' worth of air within its walls.

Dame Corby and Tchango Muttney were the first to react, diving under the table with a yelp. Blix's own colleagues were more frightened of him than we were. The Prices and Moobin responded more sensibly; steel shutters suddenly appeared across the windows and doors, closing with a *chunk-chunk-chunk* that echoed throughout the old building. Perkins dashed to the door of the dining room and peered out.

"All clear out here," he said.

"Wandering into Zambini Towers is a big risk," observed Full Price. "He must want something badly."

"He knows RUNIX and wants revenge," I said, a knot tightening in my stomach, "and we have four gig of raw crackle sitting in the Palm Court."

We tumbled out of the dining room and headed downstairs to the Palm Court, which predictably enough had a seven-headed dog with flaming eyes standing guard outside. It growled menacingly, the hair on its seven necks bristling aggressively while its fourteen front legs pawed the parquet flooring and drool dripped from its seven tongues and 294 teeth. The less well acquainted with seven-headed dogs gave out a gasp of horror, but Moobin muttered, "Amateur!" and strode through the illusory beast, which evaporated like smoke.

Once inside the Palm Court we found the excellent facsimile of Samantha Flynt working at the tear we had last seen open when Monty Vanguard failed so utterly to break the passthought. Next to her were Lady Mawgon and Monty, still stone.

"I lost my way to the restroom," said the faux Samantha as she gave a heart-melting smile.

"It's over, Blix," said Moobin.

"Step away from the Dibble," ordered Full Price, index finger at the ready. I knew that he'd never newted anyone but was itching to do so.

"It might have looked like I was frightened by that dog thing," said Tiger, "but I wasn't."

"She looks sort of familiar," said the real Samantha.

"Quark," said the Quarkbeast.

"We can negotiate your surrender," I said, stepping forward—partly to stop him from being newted. He currently had eight fingers pointed at him, and while Perkins's skills were still questionable, I knew that the Prices and Moobin could take him in an instant. I think Blix knew this, as he melted out of Samantha and back into himself. He made a move to give a slow handclap.

"DON'T MOVE A MUSCLE!" I yelled. "And *very* slowly: fingers toward the floor."

Blix smiled but didn't comply. "We can talk about this. All wizards together."

"Let him make a move on us, Jenny. I so want to take him out."

"No, Moobin. Blix? Fingers down. *Real* slowly."

He looked at us all in turn, then slowly swiveled his hands until his index fingers were pointing straight down.

"There is a passage in the *Codex Magicalis*," said Blix slowly, "which states that a wizard in trouble should always be afforded every help and assistance by every other wizard, irrespective of the trouble they may find themselves in."

"Yes," I said, "and there is another section in the *Codex* that states that any six wizards may call judgment and punishment upon any other. Tiger, go to the office. In the bottom left drawer you'll find some lead finger cuffs."

"Right," said Tiger, and dashed off.

Blix looked ill at ease. "Six wizards? You've only got four."

"Muttney and Corby joined us ten minutes ago."

"Nonsense. They are loyal only to me."

"No, we're not," came a voice from the door.

"Traitors!" Blix spat. "I'll make you pay for this."

"You won't get the chance," I told him. "We could turn you over to the king, but he'd only want to pardon you or exile you or something dumb like that. No, I think we should deal with you here and now."

"What will it be?" he said with a sneer. "A high

tower with no staircase, marooned on an island in the Barents Sea populated only by carnivorous beasts?"

"No."

"A subterranean cavern with only a misshapen goblin manservant for company?"

"You should be so lucky," I replied. "No, it would be more fitting if you were punished in a manner that would make you better understand the people you almost killed today."

"Wizards?"

"Ordinary subjects of King Snodd."

"No," he said as he realized where this was heading. "For pity's sake, don't humiliate me like that—"

"Yes," I said in as grim a voice as I could muster, "ordinary incarceration in a common jail, with ordinary criminals. No lonely tower, no force field, no seven-headed something—just stone walls, gruel, an hour of exercise a day, and only the company of thieves and villains."

"Good call," said Moobin with a smile. "Like it."

Blix glared at me as Tiger arrived with the finger cuffs. "I should have killed you when I had the chance. And I had so many chances. Do you know *why* I put you in the High North Tower rather than simply killing you? Why I allowed you to stay at liberty?"

"I've no idea," I replied. "Stupidity? Some sort of illogical Evil Dark Lord code?"

"No," he replied. "Jennifer—*I am your father!*"

There was a deathly hush as I stared at Blix open-mouthed. I had always wanted to know who my parents were but hadn't pursued it because I was frightened of what I might . . . no, hang on. This was nonsense. For a start, he looked nothing like me, and I was nothing like him.

"You're a liar," I said. "You're not my father."

"No, of course not," he said with a grin. "Nothing as hideously self-righteous as you could ever spring from a Blix—but it was worth it just to see your stupid, hopeful face."

"You'd pull that sort of joke," I said coldly, "on a foundling?"

"I think you're confusing me with someone pleasant, Jennifer."

"Actually, I don't think so. Full? Cuff him. Moobin, if he even so much as *twitches,* newt him."

"With pleasure."

Full Price edged forward, fingers at the ready. It was a tense moment. Until we had the cuffs on him, Blix was still dangerous. His eyes bored into mine with hatred, and as Full Price snapped on the first of the finger cuffs, Blix shook his head and muttered, "Bloody foundlings!"

There was a *click,* a hum, and a rising whine from somewhere deep within Zambini Towers. We felt the floor flex, and the room suddenly grew lighter and three degrees warmer. The first person to realize what was going on was the most experienced wizard in the room — Blix. The Dibble Storage Coils, brimming full with four gigashandars of wizidrical energy, had just come back online.

The passthought Lady Mawgon had devised was simpler than we had thought, and reflected her feelings for Tiger and me: *Bloody foundlings!* Blix shared that deep sense of disdain. Unwittingly, Lady Mawgon had just handed a vast amount of power to the one person who shouldn't have it.

Conrad Blix, formerly "the Amazing," was now "All Powerful."

TWENTY-SIX

The All Powerful Blix

Several things happened at once. The Prices and Moobin all let fly, and the room was suddenly filled with spells and counter-spells, weaves, dodges, burns, and reversals—so much so that the dust on the floor buzzed with static and the glass in the roof began to cloud. Those of us unversed in the Mystical Arts dived for cover.

When the noise died down, I looked cautiously from where I had hidden behind the central fountain. Tiger and Perkins were with me. The Quarkbeast was next to us, frozen in mid-leap, his mouth gaping wide and showing us a perfect array of teeth rendered in the finest granite.

"Wow," I heard Blix say, "you can do some serious mischief with four gigs of crackle at your elbow! Jennifer? Are you there?"

"Perhaps," I said, not revealing myself. I looked right and left and saw that the room had six more figures delicately realized in stone — both Prices, Patrick, Moobin, and Corby. Even Tchango Muttney had been turned to granite just as he reached the door.

"You make a run for it," said Perkins. "I'll cover you."

"And then what?"

He thought for a moment. "I don't know."

"We so almost had him," I murmured. *Blast.*"

"Language," said Tiger.

"Sorry."

I was still trying to think of a plan when I heard a young woman's voice. "All Powerful Blix. I have always loved and admired you. Take me with you."

It was Samantha. Peeking around the fountain, we saw that she had reaugmented herself back to perfect gorgeousness and was approaching Blix, who had improved himself, too. His hair was no longer streaked with gray, and he was ten years younger, four inches taller, and, by the looks of it, physically stronger. He was temporarily as powerful as any sorcerer who had ever been. Of course, he'd be back to normal once he used up the power in the Dibble, but a clever mage can do a lot with four gigashandars. A castle, a fast car, a wardrobe full of mousefur suits — you name it.

He smiled and put out his hand to take hers.

"Samantha," he said, "are you ready and willing to obey my every command?"

"Yes, yes, I shall," she replied eagerly. "For every evil genius, there must be a ludicrously beautiful woman doing apparently very little at his side."

"I see that you and I speak the same language."

"I hope so," she said demurely, "but it's been three years, and you could have made a bit more effort."

He raised an eyebrow. "More effort? To do what?"

"To learn my name. You don't pronounce the first *a*!"

She attempted to grab his fingers. It was a brave attempt but futile. In an instant there was nothing but a small and very pretty guinea pig scurrying around the floor making loud *weep-weep-weep* noises.

"What *has* the world come to," said Blix to the room in general, "when an evil genius can't even trust pretty girls who throw themselves at him?"

We ducked back down behind the fountain.

"That was brave," said Perkins.

"Jennifer," came Blix's voice again, "it's time to show yourself. It's been fun, all this back-and-forth, but I've got better things to do than monkey around with amateurs."

"I'll be out in a minute," I shouted. "I just have to do something."

"What's he going to do with us?" whispered Perkins.

"With that amount of power, almost anything he wants. We don't have a hope of vanquishing him now."

Tiger snapped his fingers. "Unless we can get someone to marry him. Vision BO55, remember? Blix's wife would be greater and more powerful than he, and ultimately be the agent of his downfall."

"Brilliant," said Perkins. "What's your plan? Marry him to a dangerously insane sorcerer with ten gig of crackle on tap?"

"It was just a thought."

"What if he were already married?" came a voice. "What if an impressionable young girl had married him in secret against her better judgment and despite her other, better suitor?"

We turned. It was Once Magnificent Boo, who had taken refuge behind an upturned table. It took a moment to figure it out. Zambini and Blix had once been close. If Boo had chosen Blix over Zambini, that would explain a lot. Maybe the fight hadn't been about the future of magic at all.

"You're Mrs. Blix?" I asked.

"When was this Vision BO55?" she responded.

I told her it had been predicted just after she had won the seven golds at the Olympics, and her jaw tightened.

She pulled her gloves off, revealing that each of her hands was missing the index finger. She looked at her hands, then at us. Then she stood up.

"Hello, Conrad," she said, and we peered cautiously over the parapet of the fountain to see what would happen next.

"Ah," he said. "Boo. You can leave. My argument is not with you."

"But mine," she replied, "is with you. I just heard that you sought a vision from Sister Yolanda and received one: that your wife—me—would be more powerful than you, and ultimately vanquish you?"

Blix swallowed nervously. "I was married. I was young. I was foolish. I was just *checking.*"

"You wanted to check I wouldn't be greater than you?"

"No," he said in a quiet voice. "I wanted to check we'd be happy."

Perkins, Tiger, and I exchanged glances. Only a fool or someone in love asks a pre-cog how things will turn out.

"And you couldn't be happy if I was better than you?"

Blix looked sheepish.

"You had me kidnapped," she said slowly as she figured it out. *"You did this to me."*

She showed him her hands, and I saw him blanch for

a moment, as even he realized just how hideously cruel he had been.

"I trusted you," Boo said, her voice rising slightly as she fought to keep herself under control. "I could have been someone. We all could have been someone. You, me, and Zambini together—a force for good in this world. You didn't just destroy me; you sabotaged a lifetime of research, discovery, and the advance of magic as a noble art. Do you have any idea what you have done?"

We looked at Blix, waiting for an answer. There wasn't one, of course.

"Yeah, well," he said with a shrug, "we've already established that I'm unpleasant, untrustworthy, and . . . and . . . and—"

"Devious?" I suggested from behind the fountain.

"Devious. Right. So what are you going to do about it, Boo? You've got nothing. Not much of a standoff, is it?"

"I'll find my fingers," she said in a low voice, "and they'll still be as powerful today as when you had them removed. And when I get them, you'll be sorry."

"You won't find them," he said with a sneer. "I made them unfindable. No one can find them. Not even I could find them."

And that was when I stood up in full view of Blix, who could have turned me to stone in a second.

"Lady Mawgon could find them," I said in a voice

cracked with fear, "with the Wizard Moobin and Full Price, with Perkins in reserve."

"Impossible!" Blix said.

"We were asked by the Mighty Shandar's agent to find a ring that was missing. A ring that didn't want to be found. But that wasn't what they were *really* after." I paused as this sank in. "I only looked as far as the ring. I never checked the small terra cotta pot that it came in."

I brought the small pot out of my bag, where it had been since the moose had oversurged, and upended it into my hand. The ring fell out first, a large ring, the sort that might fit on an index finger. Then I shook out dried dirt, a few scraps of material, and finally — several human finger bones.

Moobin was right; a ring has no power. The energy the moose had extracted had come not from the ring but from Boo's missing fingers. Her own natural energy was augmented by decades of loss, hatred, bitterness, and betrayal.

I think Blix knew the game was up, and I like to think there was just a small vestige of love in his dark heart that made him pause, lose the speed advantage and, ultimately, the battle.

Maybe deep down he knew he had to atone.

Boo grasped my elbow tightly to reconnect with the power in her lost fingers, and I felt a pulse of energy shoot down my forearm. My nails punctured my palm as my fist shut on the finger bones, but I didn't feel the pain. In an instant Boo and Blix were locked in a spell, a wall of blue light welling up between them as they tried to break down each other's defenses. They struggled, grappling with each other. The heat and light increased, a heavy wind blew up, and a moment later there was a blinding flash.

TWENTY-SEVEN

Aftermath

I may have been unconscious for a few moments; I don't know. But when I came to, Boo was brushing herself off and placing her lost bones back into the small terra cotta pot. Blix was now rendered perfectly in black granite, his last agonizing yell of pain preserved forever. Sister Yolanda's prophecy had come true. Hers always do.

"Well," said the Magnificent Boo in a chirpy voice, "I think that turned out quite favorably, don't you?"

"Yes," I said. "Yes, I think it did."

"Why do you think the Mighty Shandar wanted my fingers?"

"I don't know," I replied. "To push destiny? For more power? Maybe Shandar's getting rid of those who might challenge him when he returns. Perhaps we've yet to find out. Magic works in mysterious ways."

"It certainly does." Boo placed the small pot containing her lost fingers in her handbag, picked up her gloves, and started to walk away.

"Will you be coming back?" I asked.

"I have Quarkbeasts to feed. And they like their walkies." She gave me a smile. "Keep well, Miss Jennifer Strange."

"I will," I said. "Thank you."

She nodded and walked away.

The formerly stone Kazam staff were stretching themselves after their brief incarceration. A thousand years or eight seconds feels the same when one is stone, so I think they were very glad to see Tiger and me unchanged — and Blix in granite, of course.

"That was very, very brave, Samantha," I heard Moobin say once Tiger had explained what had happened.

"Thank you," she said, "but can I just point out that you don't pronounce the *a* . . ."

"You!" said Lady Mawgon, whose capacity to harangue me did not seem to have diminished during her imprisonment. "I am hungry. Instruct Cook to make me a cheese sandwich and a cup of tea. I shall be in my room. Don't forget to knock, and if the sandwich is unsatisfactory, I will send it back."

And she glided out of the Palm Court.

"Back to normal, eh?" said Tiger to me.

"Back to normal."

There was a lot of explaining to do to everyone, and word soon came through from Lord Tenbury that the general magic amnesty had been signed by the king. The day's spelling would not require any paperwork at all, for which I was very glad. Every sorcerer at Kazam, whether licensed or not, took advantage of this and contributed to finishing the bridge. It was completed in twenty-three minutes and was open to traffic by teatime.

Now that we knew the passthought, we could use the stored crackle to carry out much-needed repairs to Zambini Towers. By the time the Dibble Storage Coils were once again empty, the old building shone like a new pin, with a fresh coat of paint, varnished wood, and polished brass. The Palm Court was once again full of lush tropical vegetation; the central fountain, dry for more than six decades, had gurgled into life. We even restocked the wine cellar and reinstated the elevators but kept the service elevator empty and free-fall-enabled, just for fun.

Over an extended afternoon tea I had to repeat the story of the trip up to Trollvania about six times, as news of Zambini had been sparse and everyone wanted to know how he was.

At five o'clock I was in a press conference, and after that I fielded a few calls from new clients who had seen the work we did that afternoon. If things turned out well, we would have more than enough work for our sorcerers, as well as the ones we'd just inherited from iMagic.

"A busy day," said Perkins, who dropped into the office when things were finally beginning to calm down.

I smiled. "Very busy."

"Too busy for that date at the Dungeon Rooms?"

I didn't hesitate. "Not at all—I'd like that very much."

"Lobby at seven, then—and without Tiger."

"No Tiger," I said. "Promise."

So I went and took a bath and changed into my second-best dress.

I wasn't waiting in the lobby for long. Perkins arrived dressed in a suit, and dotted around the lobby were most of the residents, eager to see us walk out together.

"You're looking very lovely," he said.

"Thank you."

He held the door open.

"Wait!" It was Tiger, running from the direction of the office and holding a sheet of paper.

"I'm off-duty," I told him, "for the first time in four years."

"But—"

"No buts. Off-duty."

I smiled at Perkins as he took my arm and escorted

me outside to my Volkswagen, the Quarkbeast already sitting in the back seat with a red ribbon tied around its neck in a vain attempt to make it look less fearsome. Perkins opened the driver's door for me, and I paused.

"Perkins, would you excuse me just a moment?"

"Sure."

I dashed inside and found Tiger walking back to the office. "What's up, Tiger?"

"The Tralfamosaur escaped," he said, greatly relieved. "It's loose somewhere between here and Ross."

"Anyone eaten?"

"Two railroad workers and a fisherman."

I clapped my hands together. "Okay, we're going to need every sorcerer with a license on this one. Have everyone outside and ready in ten minutes, and fetch Emergency Pack Alpha stocked with several sarcastic light globes and a ball of enchanted string. I'm going to go change."

I found Perkins waiting for me in the lobby as I ran toward the elevators.

"I'm sorry," I said. "It's the Tralfamosaur. Do you mind if I—?"

He smiled. "Go. But we'll try this again?"

"We have lots of time," I replied.

TWENTY-EIGHT

The End of the Story

No need to panic. We caught the Tralfamosaur—eventually.

Lord Tenbury was as good as his word, and all charges against the sorcerers were dropped. None of those in the daisy chain faced as much as an interview. The king had learned his lesson and for the most part left us alone—we didn't really cross swords again until the Spoiled Royal Princess Episode, and the Fifth Troll War, of course.

The bridge at Hereford stands there still. Looking at it, you would never know that it had ever fallen down and been rebuilt, a testament to the potential of wizidrical civil engineering projects.

The Magnificent Boo never came to live at Zambini

Towers, but we saw much of her, and she continued her research into the Quarkbeast, with extraordinary results. Tchango Muttney and Dame Corby became full members of Kazam and were elevated to Amazing status the following March, the same time Lady Mawgon became Astonishing and Moobin Remarkable. iMagic was disbanded, and although we did eventually bring the mobile phone network back online, it had to wait until after we had finished reactivating medical scanners, radar, and microwave ovens.

Prince Nasil and Owen of Rhayder were grounded for a number of months until we managed to source some angels' feathers to rebuild their rugs—something that became a small adventure in itself. Mother Zenobia was returned from stone just in time to go *back* to stone for her "afternoon nap." We still see her often and value her wise counsel.

Perkins is still learning as he works, and as far as I can see, he's learning well. For her stalwart yet rash bravery during the final Blix showdown, Samantha Flynt was granted a full cadetship at Kazam "no matter how long it took." She has still to get her magic license, despite the King's Useless Brother's insistence that she should have a license anyway, "for being so utterly captivating." She has turned down his proposal of marriage sixty-seven times, proving perhaps that she is not *quite* as stupid as we think.

Tiger is still learning about running the company and, if the Great Zambini does not appear by the time I am eighteen, will take Kazam over from me then. He will be good at it, and probably better than I.

As for the Once All Powerful Conrad Blix, we donated him to the Hereford Museum, where he can still be seen to this day. His perfidious exploits are outlined for all to read, and his unseeing granite form is insulted and derided by the many schoolchildren who visit the museum. His attempt to kill half the residents of Hereford and seize the throne is often talked about, and his lack of compassion, rampant greed, and murderous intent are often compared to that of his mad evil-genius grandfather, Blix the Hideously Barbarous.

It's what he would have wanted.